Secr

'*If you are reading this you are in mortal danger. Take the book, leave now and cover your tracks. I pray you are brave at heart and of good character and, if so, read on then do what you must.*'

Charlie is not enthusiastic about going to the Edinburgh Festival with his parents—it is rather embarrassing to have a mum and dad who are acrobats. And he is not even allowed to take his PlayStation. The only thing he can do is explore the Old Town and its historic sites—especially the Underground City with its legend about a drummer boy who haunts the tunnels. It is said he can still be heard, beating his drum below the surface of the streets.

But when Charlie finds an old diary in one of the underground caverns he realizes that there is something even more terrifying and dangerous lurking under the city, something that has been imprisoned for hundreds of years, just waiting to be set free and take its revenge . . .

Jan-Andrew Henderson was born in Dundee in 1962. After graduating he travelled for several years—but wherever he went he wrote and staged plays as far apart as the Edinburgh Festival and Texas. In 1998 he settled in Scotland and set up Black Hart Storytellers, a modern and innovative storytelling company, and Black Hart Entertainment, one of the largest ghost tour companies in the country. A year later he began writing non-fiction, bringing out three books in the next three years: *The Town Below the Ground*, *The Emperor's New Kilt*, and *The Ghost that Haunted Itself*. After the birth of his son, he moved on to writing children's fiction. *Secret City* is his first novel for Oxford University Press.

Secret City

Secret City

Jan-Andrew Henderson

OXFORD
UNIVERSITY PRESS

OXFORD
UNIVERSITY PRESS

Great Clarendon Street, Oxford OX2 6DP

Oxford University Press is a department of the University of Oxford.
It furthers the University's objective of excellence in research, scholarship,
and education by publishing worldwide in

Oxford New York

Auckland Bangkok Buenos Aires
Cape Town Chennai Dar es Salaam Delhi Hong Kong Istanbul
Karachi Kolkata Kuala Lumpur Madrid Melbourne Mexico City Mumbai
Nairobi São Paulo Shanghai Taipei Tokyo Toronto

Oxford is a registered trade mark of Oxford University Press
in the UK and in certain other countries

British Library Cataloguing in Publication Data available

ISBN 0 19 271957 2

1 3 5 7 9 10 8 6 4 2

Typeset by AFS Image Setters Ltd, Glasgow

Printed in Great Britain by
Cox & Wyman Ltd, Reading, Berkshire

This book is dedicated to Sarah and Charlie.

I'd also like to acknowledge the help and support given me by Jillian and Kyle Gardiner, my mum and dad, Katherine Naish, Siobhan Reardon, Charmead Schella, Kate Sinclair, David Swift, Claire Valentine, Emily Canter, and Catriona Wilson.

Fairies, elves, pixies, leprechauns—there are many names for that elusive race of humanoids; the Little People.

Kevin Farmer: *This Strange Planet*

Many of our ancestors lived in constant fear of offending the fairies . . . they were neither cute nor adorable, but dangerous, vindictive, cruel, and not to be trusted for an instant.

Maurice Fleming: *Not of this World*

The Drummer Boy

Charlie Wilson was a quiet boy. His parents moved around a lot and he didn't have many friends, so he kept himself to himself. He spent a lot of time sitting in his room playing with his PlayStation or trying to beat his own high score on some computer game. When he grew up he wanted to be either a computer programmer or an air-traffic controller because then he'd get paid a lot to sit and press buttons all day.

'When I was young I was out having real adventures instead of fooling around with some television game,' Charlie's father said.

'When you were young, television hadn't been invented,' Charlie replied. 'Playing these games I can have totally amazing adventures. I can become anyone I want.'

And his father sighed and nodded because, secretly, he thought that didn't sound too bad at all.

He had no idea that Charlie Wilson was soon to *have* a totally amazing adventure. And that, in the process, he would become an explorer, a magician, a detective, and a grave robber.

Then, finally, he'd become a killer.

* * *

One day, just before term ended, Charlie came home to find his mother doing handstands in the hall—not that this was anything unusual, for his parents were both professional acrobats. This was a career Charlie found highly embarrassing, so he pretended to everyone that they worked in a bank. Charlie didn't much approve of his parents.

'Guess what?' his mother said, upside down. Her long dark hair brushed the hall floor.

'You found a new way to sweep?'

'Very funny.' His mother gracefully flipped herself back on to her feet. 'We've been asked to perform at the Edinburgh International Festival. Up in Scotland. There's a whole show there dedicated to physical performance.'

'You mean it's a circus,' Charlie sighed.

'Oh, it's much classier than that—not an elephant or clown in sight.' Charlie's father stuck his head out of the living room door and waggled his eyebrows. 'This might even be our chance to get famous.'

Charlie had never heard of any such thing as a famous acrobat and he certainly didn't want his parents to be the first—they'd be absolutely insufferable. And he was even more horrified to learn that they were going to take him to Edinburgh with them.

'We certainly can't leave you behind, tempting though it might be.' His father patted the boy on the shoulder. 'It'll do you good to go somewhere different. Bring you out of your shell.'

'What do you think I am?' said Charlie grumpily. 'A mollusc?'

2

'You'll love it,' said his mother, doing a somersault and knocking over the umbrella stand. 'We'll only be there three weeks, but it's the biggest arts festival in the world. There are street performers and jugglers and music and comedy and plays.'

'And all the bars stay open till three in the morning,' said his father. 'Not that that makes any difference to anything, mind you.'

'We can do family things together for a change.' His mother ruffled the boy's thick blond hair before noticing that her nail varnish wasn't quite dry. 'When we're not performing, of course. How would you like to learn to juggle?'

'I'd rather chew my own arms off,' said Charlie rubbing the pink sticky patch left on his head.

It didn't matter what he said; his parents took him to Edinburgh anyway.

In Edinburgh the City Council had shut down a narrow, disused street in the old part of the city and erected a huge fibreglass tent in the middle—it stretched from a derelict concert hall on one side of the road to a set of abandoned tenements on the other. ('Tenement' was an old Scottish word for a tall building.) This was to be the special theatre where Charlie's parents and other acrobats would perform.

Two workmen stood watching the last of the scaffolding being removed. One was barely out of school, pale and scrawny, with so much acne he looked as if he was blushing. The other was nearing retiring age, his skin brown and cracked as an oak door and his thin white hair matted with plaster dust.

3

'Just like a circus big top, eh, Jim?' the younger one said. 'Only smaller.'

Jim nodded. He had long ago run out of things to say to his companion.

'Hey! You hear aboot Harry?' the teenager continued. He seemed to dislike silence. 'Him and the lads were using a wee cellar at the bottom of those deserted flats fur their breaks—it was nice an' cosy, know? And out of sight o' the gaffer,' he added with a wink.

Jim sighed and leant on his spade. The youngster took this as a sign of interest and kept going.

'He was foolin' about wi' one of the pneumatic drills an' knocked a hole right through the cellar wall.' The youngster sniggered. 'And guess what? The lads said they found a tunnel behind it.'

The older man didn't seem surprised. 'Aye. I've heard stories aboot tunnels under these streets ever since I was wee.'

'When wuz that? Nineteen oatcake?' The teenager's snorting laugh turned into a fit of coughing. He pulled a cigarette from behind his greasy ear and lit it.

'There's a famous legend in Edinburgh,' the more experienced man continued without a change of expression, 'about a bunch of soldiers fixing up the dungeons in Edinburgh Castle who found a hidden tunnel.'

'I didnae hear about that.'

'This was two hundred years ago.'

'Oh.' The youth thought for a moment. 'I wasnae around then.'

Jim sighed and continued. 'The army wanted to know where this passage went, but it was awful small. So they took a wee boy, gave him a drum to bang and chucked him in. The lad crawled into the darkness and the soldiers followed on top, right out of the castle and down the main street.'

'Whit happened?'

'After about half a mile, the drumming stopped.'

'Maybe he went on strike.'

'Nobody knows what happened.' The older man shrugged. 'The army decided just to forget the whole thing—they hid the tunnel again and now everybody thinks it was just a daft story.' Jim held up a warning finger. 'But late at night, if there's no traffic about, you're supposed to hear phantom drumming coming from below this very street.'

'Load o' nonsense,' the teenager said cheerfully. 'Let's go an' get a mug o' tea.'

'All legends have a grain of truth in them, lad,' said Jim.

'We'll find out soon enough,' the boy grinned. 'We told the council about the tunnel and it turns out there's nae official records of it—so they offered us overtime to have a wee dig under the rest of the cellars—see if we find anything else interesting.'

'That's a bit odd, eh?' Jim said thoughtfully. 'These buildings are almost two hundred years old. They must have known about the tunnels but they still built on top of them. And there's no records, you say?'

'Guy from the council said they got destroyed about the same time the tenements went up.' The boy hefted his spade onto a skinny shoulder, impatient to get his mug of tea.

'Nothing left but legends.' The old man looked up

at the deserted windows, dark and empty as soulless eyes. He scratched his stubbled chin and frowned. 'It's like somebody, long ago, wanted what's under this street forgotten.'

The Tunnel

Once he got to Edinburgh, Charlie had to admit that he liked it—especially the historic 'Old Town'. It was built on a defensive ridge leading up to Edinburgh Castle and its tenements and stone spires towered over the rest of the city—Charlie imagined that the Old Town probably looked much the same now as it did centuries ago.

There were plenty of things to see and do in a city filled with flowering gardens, ancient courtyards, hidden alleys, and vast museums. And Charlie's mother had been right about the Edinburgh Festival—for three weeks the city's streets were packed with jugglers, magicians, unicyclists, human statues, and hundreds of other performers, all dressed in weird and wonderful costumes to promote their shows. All the same, he wished he'd been allowed to bring his PlayStation.

There was one place he *did* find fascinating and that was the theatre where his parents were performing. It was really half theatre and half big top—tent shaped but made out of fibreglass rather than fabric. Like a theatre, its walls were rigid and it had a door rather than an entrance flap. Yet it was as temporary as any circus tent—erected especially for the Edinburgh Festival and destined to be taken down again afterwards. And inside there was no stage or curtains because, as his father explained, this theatre was built just for *acrobatic* performances.

'None of your Shakespeare nonsense here, Charlie,' said his father happily. 'No men in tights running around shouting "*Thou hast killed me, naughty knave,*" and waving plastic swords.' He pointed proudly to the girders, wires, and poles that towered above them. 'When acrobats perform it's a matter of life and death. There's *real* danger here.'

'And that's a *good* thing?'

Charlie's father shrugged. 'It's better than working in a bank.'

In fact, there was more danger in this particular big top than he could possibly have imagined.

'You can come and watch us practise if you like.' Charlie's father was still staring longingly upwards. 'Perhaps, one day, you can be part of the act.'

'I've already seen you practise,' Charlie muttered. He had lost count of the number of coffee tables his parents had broken leaping around the living room. The boy looked up at the ridged fibreglass roof. 'It doesn't look all that dangerous to me,' he said. 'The high wire isn't all that high, is it?' He pointed to a tightrope a few feet above their heads with a criss-crossing mesh dangling just below it. 'Anyway, there's a net.'

Charlie's father looked down at his son.

'That's not the high wire,' he said laughing. 'Watch this.' He took a remote control from a nearby table, pointed it at the roof and clicked a button. There was a loud hissing noise and a crack of white appeared high above in the centre of the structure. The boy flinched.

With an electronic hum, the two halves of the big top roof slid slowly back from the middle, like a huge mouth yawning, until the building was completely open to the sky. There was another hiss and vertical poles, forty feet apart and with a metal tightrope stretched between them, extended up and up through the gap that had been the roof and into the open air—until the tightrope looked thin as thread.

'*That's* the high wire,' said Charlie's father in a whisper.

'All right,' Charlie admitted, taking the remote control and inspecting it. 'I'm impressed.' His stomach tightened at the thought of his parents balancing so high on the thinnest of wires—but he did like gadgets with buttons.

The other thing that fascinated Charlie about the theatre was where it had been erected. It was in one of the narrow little roads that the inhabitants called 'wynds'—which sloped steeply down from the High Street, the main street of the Old Town, into the Cowgate—a run-down area festooned with pubs, much to the delight of Charlie's father. The boy liked the way that the big top was fastened to buildings on either side rather than being secured by guy ropes hammered into the ground like a normal circus tent.

'They look like an ordinary bunch of flats, don't they?' Charlie's father had said with a wink, pointing to the abandoned and crumbling tenements. 'Well, they're not.'

These tenements happened to have been built in front of a gigantic bridge but they were so tall that they made the structure behind almost invisible. This 'South Bridge' was constructed in the eighteenth century so horses and carts could cross the Old Town without risking the steep slopes of the Cowgate valley. Under the massive bridge arches hundreds of stone chambers linked by passages had been constructed—all easily accessible until the tenements had been built in front to hide them. These chambers were supposed to be used as storage vaults but, according to Charlie's dad, people had ended up living there. In fact, Edinburgh was so overcrowded that the citizens even dug tunnels into the steep sides of the Old Town ridge—and then inhabited those too.

'You swallow a guide book?' Charlie asked, frowning.

'They called it the Underground City,' said Charlie's father in a whisper. 'The places where the very poorest people lived. It was a long time ago, mind you, and it's all been built over or hidden, so lots of local people think it never really existed.' His father tapped the side of his nose. 'But I know it does.'

'Oh yeah? *How* do you know?' Charlie was suddenly interested—after all, he'd been playing *Tomb Raider* for most of the spring. Charlie's father looked surprised—it wasn't often he said something that his son actually wanted to hear.

'Because the construction crew setting up the big top dug a bit of it up by mistake,' he said, taking the boy by the arm. 'Come and look at this.'

He led his son over to a dark corner of the big top where a door the boy hadn't noticed lurked in the shadows. His father opened it and they stepped into a short corridor. There was grubby plaster peeling from the walls and wooden slats and bare wires dangled from the roof.

'You can go from the big top right into the abandoned buildings and behind that are the bridge vaults themselves.' His father opened a second door and ushered Charlie through. 'It's like walking back in time.'

They now stood in a musty vault with a low roof and uneven brickwork—it looked very, very old. The chamber contained a pile of shovels and drills, a folding table covered in dirty cups, and a large portable generator which gave off an evil hum and smelt of burnt toast. The theatre construction crew had obviously used the little cellar to store their equipment and have tea breaks.

Charlie's father moved a mop, bucket, and some plastic safety helmets stacked against the side of the generator. On impulse he tried juggling three of the helmets but one bounced off the roof and hit the boy on the head.

'Sorry, Charlie,' said his father. 'Ceiling's a bit too low for that.'

Charlie wasn't listening. Behind the mop and helmets was a ragged hole in the ancient brick wall and, even in the dim light of the makeshift bulb swinging from the storeroom ceiling, he could see there was a tunnel on the other side.

'Is that . . . ?'

'Part of the Underground City? I think it has to be.' Charlie's father switched on a lamp attached to one of the safety helmets and shone it into the hole—a narrow, moss-lined passage stretched into the distance as far as the beam could reach. 'The

11

workmen building the tent found it.' He knelt down beside Charlie and looked into the tunnel. 'I bet nobody's been in there for a hundred years or more—it's way too small for any of the workers to fit inside—have you seen how many sandwiches these guys eat?' He stood up and began to practise juggling with the helmets again. 'I hear Edinburgh Council want them to excavate the place properly.'

The boy stuck his head into the hole. There was a stale smell similar to the one inside his parents' fridge at home—his mother and father weren't too big on cleaning.

'I bet *I* could fit in here.' Charlie waved his hand about in the empty space.

'Don't even think about it,' warned his father, dropping the helmets with a crash. 'I heard a story in the pub about a little boy who was forced into one of these abandoned passages and never came out again. They say you can hear his ghost drumming under the ground. I forget why he had a drum in the first place.' He scratched his head. 'To be honest I don't remember much about that whole night.' He put the mop and helmets back to hide the hole once more. 'Don't think of going down there anyway.'

Charlie's father was sure his son had no intention of venturing anywhere near the tunnel again—he'd rather sit in his room and play video games than have a *proper* adventure. He forgot that Charlie hadn't been able to bring his PlayStation with him.

The boy had already made a fateful decision. If he couldn't play *Tomb Raider* in the comfort of his own home, he would give the real thing a try—after all, it was better than wandering around Edinburgh on his own. Why, he might even discover treasure in the tunnel or find a gold mine or something!

If Charlie had thought more carefully about his computer games, he would have realized that there is a sort of rule regarding hidden treasure.

That rule is this: wherever you find buried treasure, you are also likely to find something horrible guarding it.

The Juggler

Visiting a new place has an odd effect on some people. Perhaps it's because nobody knows who they are or their routine is changed or maybe the air is just different. Whatever the reason, they sometimes find themselves acting quite out of the ordinary, and that's exactly what was happening to Charlie Wilson. The very next day he got up long before his mother and father and went down to breakfast on his own. The family were staying at a local guest house and it was so early the boy was the first one into the little dining room. The walls were covered in tartan wallpaper and faded pictures of funnily shaped birds.

'Hello there, sonny! Would you like a wee spot of Scottish breakfast?' A plump waitress with a beaming smile appeared at his table.

'Scottish breakfast?'

'Aye. Bacon, sausage, fried egg, fried tomato, fried bread, mushrooms, potato scone, black pudding, fruit pudding, haggis, hash browns, beans, chips, tea, toast and jam.'

Charlie swallowed hard. 'Do you have any Weetabix? I was hoping to be able to move today.'

'We've got porridge,' said the waitress without

14

batting an eyelid. 'It's grey and lumpy. Just like Weetabix.'

'I'll just have a glass of orange juice, thanks.'

Charlie's parents liked to think they were very modern, as well as being rather busy, and so they allowed their son to pretty much come and go as he pleased. They had given him a mobile phone in case of emergencies but they were sure he would never talk to strangers or go anywhere that looked even slightly dangerous.

'We should be thankful he's so ordinary, I suppose,' Charlie's mother said to her husband. 'When I was a child I got into all sorts of trouble.'

'A child?' Charlie's father sighed. 'We got thrown out of the pub last week after you did the splits on the bar. But you're right, Charlie's not like us—he's a sensible boy.'

Which shows you that even parents can be wrong. After breakfast Charlie headed straight for the big top, intending to explore the mysterious tunnel.

His father had given the boy a key for the theatre in case he wanted to come and watch the rehearsals—acrobats couldn't exactly come down from their trapeze to answer the door. Charlie had no desire to watch his parents go through their act for he was convinced that, one day, they'd fall and break every bone in their bodies. But he knew that the big top was deserted in the mornings—his parents hated to get up early and Charlie supposed that all performers were the same.

As soon as he was inside the big top he made his way to the shadowy door at the back, crossed through the abandoned building and entered the bridge vault. He moved the mops and buckets away from the passage, took one of the construction helmets, switched on the light and fastened it on his head. It was far too big, but Charlie's thick hair acted like a cushion that stopped the hard-hat falling over his eyes.

Then he looked into the tunnel opening. The passage was damp and dark and he had no idea what was at the end of it. There might be an underground cliff or a bogeyman or, worse, the tunnel might get smaller and smaller until he found himself trapped for ever. On the other hand there might be some sort of forgotten treasure down there, like they found under the pyramids, and what sort of super-computer could he buy *then*?

He put his arm tentatively into the dank opening and a cold draught raised goose bumps on his flesh. He shivered violently all over.

'Who do I think I am, Indiana Jones?' Charlie withdrew his arm and backed away from the hole shaking his head. 'I wouldn't crawl down there if my life depended on it!' He stood up and hurried back to the big top again still shivering from his sudden attack of the heebie-jeebies. 'I'll go find a computer store instead,' he muttered. 'See what the latest releases are.' He stopped in surprise, halfway to the outside door. 'Oh . . . er. Hello.'

In the middle of the theatre, shrouded in shadow, stood a girl in a short velvet dress. She was juggling—not three balls or four, but six or even seven bright green orbs, and they glittered intermittently as they spun around her back and over her head.

'Hi there.' The girl turned and spoke without missing a beat. She looked about Charlie's age and her eyes and dress were as bright a green as her juggling balls.

'I didn't think anyone performed here in the morning,' Charlie said.

'I'm not a performer,' the girl replied, her hands a blur of motion. 'But my father's a magician. I'm practising to be as good as him.'

'Really?' Charlie pointed to the spinning balls. 'That's not magic, though, is it? That's just juggling.'

The girl arched an eyebrow and let her arms drop to her side. The balls scattered across the theatre floor like startled frogs and vanished under the audience chairs. Charlie grimaced; perhaps that hadn't been the right way to start the conversation. 'My parents are one of the acts here too,' he said pleasantly, trying to start again. 'They're acrobats.'

The girl nodded as if she already knew. 'Do you think *you'll* ever be as good as them?'

'Me?' Charlie laughed awkwardly. 'I don't want to be an acrobat.'

The girl looked up at the trapeze dangling above. 'I suppose. It must be frightening up there.'

'It's not that I'm afraid,' Charlie said, embarrassed by the misunderstanding. 'But why do something dangerous just for the sake of it?'

'Is that why you decided not to explore the tunnel?'

'Eh?'

'I've seen it too.' The girl gave a sly smile that Charlie didn't much like. 'In the broom cupboard at the back of the theatre. It's very dark.'

Charlie felt himself go red. 'What makes you think I'm interested in exploring some stupid tunnel?'

'You've got a hard-hat with a light on your head.'

'Yeah. Well, I *was* going to check it out,' the boy blustered. 'I . . . er . . . just came back to make sure the theatre door was locked.'

'It is,' said the girl. 'I'll keep an eye on the place while you finish exploring, don't worry.' She walked over and straightened his helmet. 'My name's Lily.'

'I'm Charlie,' replied Charlie. At a loss for anything else to say, he sighed and headed back towards the storage vault.

Charlie hunkered down beside the generator, staring into the tunnel once more—surely he wasn't going to go in there just to prove to some weird girl that he wasn't scared?

Then the boy thought of his parents. He had never understood why they wanted to risk their lives swinging high above the ground—he had asked his father once but he had just laughed gently.

'I don't want to grow dull and fat working as some banker or salesman, Charlie,' he tried to explain. 'You only live once, so you may as well *really* live.' At the time Charlie hadn't understood what that meant but now he wondered if, for once, his father might be proud that he was taking a chance. Anyway, he had his mobile phone if he got into trouble.

With a deep breath, Charlie knelt down and slid head first into the tunnel.

The moss on the walls was surprisingly dry and spongy, which made crawling easy, and after a few

18

dozen yards he realized the little channel was beginning to widen. Another fifty feet and the tunnel opened out into a wider passage, this one large enough for Charlie to stand.

'Whoa! I really am in the Underground City,' he whispered to himself, looking around in awe. The flashlight on his helmet lit up an ancient curved roof, dripping with thin fingers of hardened salt. 'This is well and truly the stupidest thing I've ever done.'

He might be taking a chance, but Charlie Wilson certainly wasn't stupid. He took a piece of chalk from his pocket (he had bought a packet especially the day before) and marked a crumbling but readable number one on the chamber wall. Then he set off down the larger passage. He passed several openings leading into vaults of different sizes and the tunnel itself twisted left then right but, every time he turned, Charlie chalked another number so that he would be able to find his way back.

'Lara Croft was never smart enough to do this,' he said proudly, just before he tripped and fell flat on his face. The mobile phone flew out of his shirt pocket and bounced away into the dark and, as Charlie scrabbled after it, his helmet bumped against the wall of the tunnel and his outstretched arm vanished into a hole between the wall and the floor. He withdrew it with a shriek just in case some big rat or land-octopus was lurking inside.

'For goodness' sake!' he panted, once he had calmed down a bit. 'How many hidden holes are in this blasted place?' He sat up and played the headlight over the little opening which was no more than a few inches long, obscured by dirt and loose rubble.

'That's just great! I couldn't have aimed the phone down there if I was a champion darts player—how am I going to explain this to Mum and Dad?' The answer, of course, was that he couldn't. He was going to have to try and rescue his mobile. The hole was half-hidden behind bricks and short straps of wood and Charlie began to move the debris to see if he could make a space big enough to reach into properly. Soon, he realized the gap was going to be large enough to fit his head and shoulders through and, though he really didn't like *that* idea, it meant he could actually see where the mobile had gone. After a few deep breaths he clenched his fists and stuck his head into the hole.

'Would you look at that!'

The light on his hard-hat lit up a small stone stairway leading down into the darkness. His mobile phone must have bounced all the way down to the bottom. Charlie was aware that, bit by bit, he was going further than he had ever intended.

'I'm brave. I'm brave, I'm brave. My mum and dad are brave and I can be brave too,' the boy chanted, fastening the helmet strap tighter with trembling fingers. 'Who am I kidding? I'm just a lot dumber than I thought.' Then he crawled right through the widened hole, fumbled his way to his feet and made his way cautiously down the stairs.

At the bottom was another passage; damp, with an uneven floor that sloped gently downwards. Charlie picked up his phone which was lying in the middle of the tunnel then, on impulse, carried on down the hill. Despite himself, the boy found he was thrilled as well as frightened and he understood for the first time how his parents must feel swinging around on their trapeze. He was a bit disappointed, in fact, when the tunnel eventually opened out into a large vault that seemed to signal the end of his journey. Charlie swung the light around but the doorway he stood in was both the entrance and exit to the chamber.

The vault wasn't completely empty—a large pyramid-shaped wooden frame and a rusty iron hook leaned against one wall, there was a mound of rocks in the far corner, and a built-up circle of stone in the middle. Charlie walked over to the brick circle, which was about waist height, and bent his head to shine the torch down into it. The beam lit up a thick layer of ash and lumpy grey remains of what must have once been coal.

'Looks like someone's been having a barbecue.' Charlie raised an eyebrow. 'Wouldn't be *my* choice of place for a picnic.'

He turned and walked towards the smaller pile of stones. Though it was no more than a heap of rocks it looked as if it had been put there deliberately. He hesitated for a few seconds, then threw caution to the wind.

'The last time I came across a pile of stones it was hiding something.' The boy bent down and began to remove the rocks. 'Doesn't seem right to come all this way and not see what's under this lot. Especially if it's a chest full of jewels.'

The stones were piled on top of a rotting wooden board and, once Charlie had uncovered most of the plank, he slid it aside. Underneath was a blackened hollow cylinder of metal the size of an oil drum—it looked as if it had been rammed into a hole in the floor. Charlie peered inside and a grin spread across

21

his dusty face. At the bottom of the cylinder was a square object wrapped in dark cloth. It looked as if it might be some kind of box.

'Treasure!' breathed Charlie. 'About time too.' Lying flat on the floor, he reached into the metal-lined hole, grasped the coarse cloth and pulled it towards him. It was certainly a package of some kind, wrapped in the crumbling remains of what looked suspiciously like a huge leather glove. With trembling hands, the boy unpeeled the leather but inside there was only a tatty book with a faded vellum cover.

'A book,' the boy sighed. 'If I wanted a book I could have gone to the library.' He gingerly opened the fragile cover and a slip of folded paper fell out. He couldn't tell from the light of the torch but he guessed it was yellow with age, for it crackled when he picked it up.

'A treasure map! Of course!' He unfolded the paper and bent his helmet closer to see what was written there. The words were hand scripted but the letters were large and thick, making it easy to read, even in the dim torchlight.

If you are reading this you are in mortal danger. Take the book, leave now and cover your tracks. I pray you are brave at heart and of good character and, if so, read on then do what you must.

Charlie sat bolt upright.

'Mortal danger?' he gasped. 'What does it mean, mortal danger?'

Then the tapping began.

It was very soft and very faint as if it were a long way down, somewhere under the floor. Charlie's eyes widened and he sprang to his feet. Already the rapping was growing louder and it was getting faster too. Though it still sounded far off, there was no doubt in the boy's mind.

The noise was heading this way.

The blood drained from Charlie's face and his bravado evaporated—he began to back out of the vault, stuffing the book into his shirt as he went. The rapping was more like a drumming now, much louder and definitely heading in his direction. And it was approaching fast.

Charlie Wilson turned and ran.

His journey back to the surface was little more than a blur, for the terrified boy ran like he had never run before, his breath hammering in his ears and the light on his head swirling sinister shadows across the passages. The chalk marks flew past, five then four then three then two then one. He sped through the corridors, bouncing off the walls and stumbling over loose rocks until he plunged back into the little tunnel, ignoring the scrapes on his hands as he frantically scrambled the last hundred yards. He didn't slow down until he had burst into the tool-filled vault and every mop, bucket, and teacup had been piled back in front of the tunnel entrance.

Charlie took the helmet from his head and placed it on the vault floor with the others—his hands were shaking so badly, he could hardly switch off the light on the front. He sat trembling on the floor, his chest heaving.

'Thank God I didn't have the full Scottish breakfast,' he panted. 'I'd still be down there.'

He got unsteadily to his feet and opened the door leading back to the theatre.

'Nobody, and I mean *nobody*, will ever make me

go back into that tunnel,' he promised, taking one last look at the covered-up hole. 'I'll never set foot in that place again as long as I live.'

But, though he meant every word, Charlie Wilson couldn't have been more wrong.

The Book

Lily was still juggling when Charlie staggered back into the theatre—he could have sworn for a second that she had at least a dozen balls in the air and what looked like a couple of mice as well. At the sound of the boy's wheezing the whirling objects vanished into some hidden pocket that jugglers always seem to have. Lily smiled innocently.

'Ah, you're back. Anything interesting down there?'

'Interesting?' Charlie slapped at his jeans and a cloud of white dust rose into the air. 'I heard the ghost of that little drummer boy! The one that's supposed to haunt the place. My heart almost stopped.'

He began to tell Lily about the drumming but, to his annoyance, the little girl started to laugh. She held up a hand to stop him.

'Charlie, there's a group of council workmen digging under the tenements from the opposite side of the bridge,' she said with a laugh. 'I saw them going to work this morning. You probably heard them drilling.'

'It sounded like drumbeats to me,' the boy scowled. 'I've never been so scared.'

'A phantom drummer, eh? You should have stuck around—the rest of the band might have turned up.'

Charlie ignored her sarcasm and pulled the book from under his shirt, releasing another cloud of dust. 'Anyway, I found this.'

'Really? Let me see.' Lily took the book and opened it. She looked intrigued. 'It's hand written—the date inside the cover says 1824.' She turned a page and read a little more. 'It's the journal of somebody called William Makepeace.'

'Like a diary?'

'Exactly.'

'Is it a joke? Some kind of hoax?'

Lily shook her head. 'There are parts of the Underground City that have been sealed for almost two centuries and this book's definitely old—see how crackly the paper is.' She peered over the top of the pages at Charlie. 'What are you looking so unhappy about?'

'I suppose this is real too?' The boy unfolded the note and handed it to Lily. 'It was inside the front page.'

'It's the same type of paper.' She read the message and looked up at him with her eyes sparkling. 'This is great!'

'Yeah. Fantastic. Especially the part about me being in mortal danger.' Charlie pointed to the offending sentence. 'What do you think it means?'

'Don't you see?' Lily said excitedly. 'The note's a warning to stop people going any further.'

'It worked then,' Charlie snorted. 'I came back soon as I read it.'

'But think! Why would anybody leave a note like that?' Lily waved the scrap of paper under Charlie's nose. 'I bet it's 'cause there's something really important hidden down there, see? And only the stout of heart will be able to find it!' Lily nodded as if this made perfect sense. 'That note's a clue but also a warning, see? Treasure!' A look of horror suddenly crossed her face. 'What if those council workers are heading towards it?'

'The speed most council workers work, they'll never get there.'

'You said the note was inside the book.' Lily was obviously swept up in her grand idea. 'Maybe the book says where the treasure is buried.'

'You are getting *totally* carried away.' Charlie held up his hands. 'It's just some old diary, that's all. We should give it to a museum or something before it gets damaged.'

'Well, we *could* do that.' Lily smiled a dazzling smile. 'But it wouldn't do any harm to read it first. Eh? Where's your sense of adventure?'

'I left it in the tunnel.'

'Look, it would only take a couple of days to read through the book. If there's nothing about treasure, you can hand it over to anyone you like.'

'And if there is?'

Lily shrugged. 'Then . . . we can decide what to do next!'

'Oh. Well, since you've got it all worked out.' Charlie gave a sigh of exasperation that somehow turned into a laugh halfway through. Lily laughed as well.

'C'mon, Charlie. It *is* quite exciting,' she said, nudging him.

'I suppose I could take it back to the guest house and have a look, but didn't they write really boring books in those days? With big long sentences?' Charlie took the diary back from Lily and opened it. 'I'm not really into reading. I like computer games.'

Lily snorted. Charlie scanned the first page, scowling with concentration. His frown deepened as he read out loud.

This iz the jurnal of myself, William Makepeace, aged about twelve, (tho I am not sure which year I was born, for I am an orphan) in which I am determinned to tell of my life and adventurz, since it is my grate desire to someday write a book of great importanse.

'I knew it!' Charlie groaned. 'I've written school essays that were shorter than his first sentence. And who taught him to spell?'

'If he was an orphan in the Underground City, he probably taught himself.' Lily arched a sarcastic eyebrow. 'Think you could do that?' The boy ignored her and began to read again.

I lived in the Canongate poorhouse until I found I was to be apprentised to MacPherson the Sweep—who wuz well known for his ill treetment of boys in his employ. He would send them up the narrowest chimneys and, shood they become stuck, would lite fires under them to perswade them out.

'Ouch!' Charlie paused. 'He's got to be making this up. Nobody's life is this bad.'

Lily looked solemn. 'In those days everybody's life was that bad. Unless they had money.'

'Well, some things never change.' The boy smiled thinly and began to read again.

One night I escaped by leeping from the poorhouse roof into a drift of snow and remaining buried until after dark. Finally, half dead with cold, I made my way to the Underground City where all manner of criminals reside and now make my living by means that I am ashamed to menshun . . .

'Wow.' Charlie looked up from the book in astonishment. 'This guy's had some life, and I'm only on the first page. I wonder what he did that he's so ashamed of.'

'Read the journal and you'll probably find out.'

'It's too difficult,' the boy protested. 'I'll never get through it.'

'Everyone has a story worth hearing,' Lily said. 'You just need to be able to picture it.' She held out a fist. 'Maybe I can help.'

She uncurled her fingers, blew across her palm, and a cloud of glittering dust circled the boy's head.

'What are you doing!' Charlie waved his arms about, scattering the shining haze. 'I got asthma, you know!'

'It's imagination. To help you read the book.'

'It's glitter, Lily.' Charlie held up a sparkly hand in disgust. 'Now I look like a girl.'

'As you were so quick to point out, I'm only a juggler.' Lily shrugged. 'What do you want me to do? Pull a rabbit out of my . . . '

'I'll read the book. All right?' The boy stuffed the journal back inside his shirt. 'I'll let you know how far I've got by tomorrow. Where do you stay? What's your phone number?' He tapped his shirt pocket proudly. 'I have a mobile.'

Lily gestured to the theatre behind her. 'You can find me right here, every morning.'

'Suit yourself.' Charlie went to the door and unlocked it. He paused with his key in the lock and turned back.

'See this mortal danger stuff? Just what kind of mortal danger do you think . . . ?'

But Lily was gone.

The Graveyard

After dinner at the guest house Charlie's parents got ready to go to the big top and perform their act.

'Do you want to come and watch?' said his father, pulling on a pair of yellow spangled tights.

'I think I'll stay in and read.' Charlie shook his head. 'Erm, you're not going to walk through town dressed like that?'

'Don't worry, Charlie, everyone will be staring at your mother.' Charlie's mother appeared to be wearing nothing more than three ostrich feathers. 'And you don't need to wait up—we thought we might go for a drink after the show. That's if we don't plunge to our deaths from the high wire. Hah. Only joking.'

As soon as his parents were gone, Charlie pulled the diary from his bag, flopped onto his bed and began to read. William Makepeace had close, shaky handwriting and that made his long and badly spelt sentences even more difficult to read.

My best frend and constant companyun is a boy a little older than I, Duncan MacPhail, who it was my grate fortune to meet, for his strenth is admirable and his bravery beyond question and it was he who perswaded me to give up my dishonorable profeshun.

Charlie felt his eyes drooping already—hadn't this boy ever heard of full stops? He tried to remember what Lily had said about using his imagination and concentrating on the story rather than the words. And Charlie had to admit, he wanted to know what this William Makepeace did that was so terrible—apart from not learning to punctuate sentences. He looked at the book again.

I was sitting in Greyfriars graveyard when I met Duncan for the first time, a fine spring day when the trees were heavie with white and pink blossums.

Charlie tried ignoring the writing and concentrating on what the writer was actually saying. He pictured ornate gravestones, stately trees ruffled by a cool spring breeze. Then the strangest thing happened. In his head, he could suddenly *see* a small boy sitting on a flat tombstone and writing in a book . . .

*   *   *

William Makepeace looked up as a scented blossom drifted past his head and landed on the vellum-covered journal balanced between his knees. Two hundred yards away, through the scattered gravestones, he could see a group of mourners in black frock coats and tall stovepipe hats attending a funeral. The boy watched them out of the corner of his eye then took a quill pen and an inkpot from his pocket, dipped in the nib and carefully made some notes.

A shadow fell across the flat tombstone on which he sat and he looked up in surprise. Three angry looking youths, one holding a stout club, stood over him—their burly forms blocking out the sun.

'We know what you're up to, pal.' One of the youths slammed the stick down on the flat stone an inch from the boy's knee. The mourners did not look round. 'You're going to wish you'd never set foot in this graveyard.'

'Now then, I'm already thinking it was a bad idea,' the boy said pleasantly, shutting the book. 'So I'll be on my way, gents, and we'll say no more about it.'

'Think you're clever, don't you?' The largest of the three boys nodded to his ragged companions. 'Grab his arms. I'm going tae teach this wee sod a lesson.'

As the toughs moved forward to seize the boy they heard a cough from behind a nearby tree and a tall youth stepped into the sunlight.

'I dinnae think that three big lads against one wee one is fair, no matter what he's done,' the stranger said calmly. His hair was long and black and a thick tartan plaid was draped over his shoulder then fastened round his waist with an ornate pin. His strange attire marked him out as a highlander—not a common sight in a city which still treated the fierce clans of northern Scotland with fear and mistrust. He kept himself between the sun and his assailants, so that his features were difficult to make out.

'This is no' your fight, friend.' The largest youth stepped forward menacingly, shading his eyes with his hand. 'Go about your business and leave us tae ours.'

'I don't mind if he joins in,' said William Makepeace. 'I think it would even up the odds nicely, as a . . . '

One of the gang lashed out, the back of his calloused hand catching Makepeace a glancing blow on the temple and knocking him backwards off the tombstone. Without a second's hesitation, the highlander launched himself forward, head down and arms spread wide—his shoulder crashed into the gang leader's chest and his outstretched fists slammed into the stomachs of the henchmen on either side. Next moment, all three toughs were on the ground gasping for air and the highlander was standing above them brandishing the stick. In his other hand a small but deadly-looking knife had appeared.

'Go on, get out of here before I cut ye.' He motioned towards the cemetery's iron gates and the gang got unsteadily to their feet and ran. The knife vanished into the highlander's tunic and he helped the little boy to his feet.

'Up ye get, wee man. Are ye all right?' He bent down again and retrieved the fallen book.

'I'm fine, thank you, and most indebted to you for saving me.' The boy held out his hand. 'My name's William Makepeace, but my friends call me Peazle. So do my enemies, for that matter. I obviously have quite a few.'

The highlander shook the proffered hand. 'Duncan MacPhail from Aftonhouse. I dinnae have any enemies.' He smiled. 'At least, not alive.'

'Then I'll count you a friend,' said Peazle. 'May I have my journal back?'

'This is a funny kind of book now, isn't it?' Duncan opened the journal and looked at the first page. 'I've been watching you write in it and yet there's nothing here.' He flicked through the remaining pages. 'Until you get tae the back, that is—then there's a map of the cemetery.' He motioned to the crowd of mourners, clustered round the open grave like unhappy shadows. 'And you've made a wee tick, marking the spot where that funeral is taking place.'

'It's my hobby,' the boy said casually. 'Funeral spotting.'

The highlander's eyes narrowed. 'It's my guess that you work for the Resurrection Men and that's why thon wee gang wished you harm.' He looked at the stout stick then back at Peazle. 'I heard stories of such a thing but I never really believed they were true.'

The Resurrection Men were the most despised of the city's many criminals—for they stole bodies from graveyards and sold them for unscrupulous scientists at Edinburgh University to experiment on. To avoid suspicion they often employed children as lookouts or had them mark out the sites of recently buried corpses. Then these bodysnatchers could return at night and rob the grave without falling over a dozen headstones in the dark.

Peazle was quick to defend himself. 'You think it's easy for an orphan living in this city? I have to eat, you know.' He angrily snatched the book from the larger boy. 'I pick pockets too, I might as well tell you. It's either that or get sent up some chimney for a living, or maybe suffocate down a Lothian mine opening trapdoors for the coal carts.'

The highlander placed a hand on the smaller boy's shoulder. 'Calm down, my friend. I know what it's like tae go hungry myself—I was forced to come down from the highlands because there's nae work to be had in the north.' He spat on the ground in anger. 'I've been here over a week and I must admit I'm faring no better.'

'No luck?'

'Oh, I have a job in an iron foundry where I work from six in the morning till eight at night for a few pennies. I sleep in a doorway because there are nae lodgings to be had.' The pickpocket could see that Duncan's piercing blue eyes were ringed by dark circles and his fine cheekbones were made even sharper by exhaustion—it suddenly occurred to Peazle that his new friend wasn't nearly as old as he first appeared. He might only be a couple of years older than the pickpocket himself—perhaps fourteen or fifteen. The highlander looked around at the laden boughs and lush green grass.

'I like it here because it's the only place in this overcrowded hellhole of a city where I can get a wee bit of peace,' he said.

Peazle could see what he meant. Though dirty tenements surrounded the high walls of Greyfriars, the graveyard held only the funeral party, a courting couple, and a few disrespectful urchins playing hide and seek. Tranquillity like that was rare in overcrowded Edinburgh, for famine and unsympathetic landowners had forced wave after wave of immigrants from the Scottish and Irish countryside to move to the cities. The population of the Old Town had doubled in the last thirty years.

'I seen a hawk here yesterday,' said Duncan. 'A white one wi' black tips on each wing—I've ne'er seen anything like it before. Didnae look right in such a dirty sky.' The highlander grabbed a falling blossom and sniffed at it—but no fragrance could block out the smell of coal smoke and sewage that permeated the city.

'I come here a lot myself,' said the pickpocket. 'Not just to spy on funerals,' he added quickly. He patted the gravestone on which he had been sitting. 'I always sit here, on the grave of Allan Ramsay. He was a great poet, you know, and a man of learning, and yet he started off as a humble shepherd, so I heard.'

'Nothing wrong with being a shepherd,' said Duncan with a scowl.

'Listen, you helped me,' the little pickpocket said. 'I'd like to return the favour. If you've nowhere to stay then you're welcome to lodge with me for a while.'

Duncan thought for a second, then he leaned behind a gravestone and picked up a small knapsack. 'Your hospitality is worthy of a highlander himself and I gladly accept. Where do you stay?'

'The Underground City.'

'That sounds powerful grim.'

'So does sleeping in a doorway. C'mon.'

He led Duncan out of the graveyard, up the Old Town ridge onto the High Street. For a few minutes they pushed their way through the crowds thronging between the bristling tenements until Peazle turned down a narrow and steeply sloping sewage-filled alley.

'The South Bridge,' said Peazle as they neared the bottom. 'Home sweet home.'

The boys stood in the shadow of the bridge's

towering pillars—its grimy brick flanks studded with openings leading to internal vaults: chambers which had been designed to hold goods and wares but, because of Edinburgh's horrific overcrowding, now held people. The tenements that would eventually hide the vault entrances had not yet been built and Peazle and the highlander simply stepped from the street into the interior of the bridge. They made their way through a series of dark vaults and narrow passages lit by dirty spluttering candles. After a while, their eyes grew accustomed to the murky light and the boys could make out vagabonds and beggars huddled in some of the darkened corners.

'This is my vault.' Peazle finally pointed to a smoky chamber where three men were playing cards by candlelight. 'It's smelly and dark and you might get murdered in your bed but at least it's dry.' There was a squelch as he stepped through the doorway. 'Well, dry-ish.'

'It smells tae high heaven.' The highlander wrinkled his nose. 'You actually pay for this?'

'I pay Merry Andrew.' Peazle lowered his voice and indicated one of the card players. The man slowly rose to his feet—once he was standing, he had to stoop to avoid hitting his head on the roof. 'He's the biggest, so the vault belongs to him.' The little pickpocket turned to the rough looking man—his face was a rash of pock marks and grey stubble, except for where a large scar ran from ear to chin. 'Merry, this is Duncan MacPhail from the highlands. I want to share my space with him for a while.'

Merry Andrew looked far from merry—in fact, he looked as if he could tear most men apart with his bare hands and was in the mood to do it.

'Oh, really? And suppose I don't want Duncan MacPhail in my vault?' he growled, his voice broken by a lifetime of loud cursing and cheap grog. 'You think this place isn't crowded enough?' He towered over the two boys. 'I reckon I'll throw Duncan out of my vault and charge you double for even suggesting it.'

'Then Duncan might come back in the middle of the night and cut off your ears while you sleep.' The highlander spoke softly but the small knife glinted in his hand once more. 'If you're going tae make enemies so easily, it's better tae keep them close so you can see what they're up tae.'

There was a stunned silence. The other card players looked at each other and gave a low whistle. Merry Andrew glowered. Then he half-smiled. Then he laughed out loud.

'Well spoken, highlander,' he said, slapping Duncan on the back. 'I like your spirit. Ha'penny a week and you can stay. I collect the money prompt each Friday.'

Peazle finally let his breath out.

Later that night Merry Andrew and his companions went to the local tavern to play dice and the highlander and the pickpocket sat in the candlelight talking.

'Where did you get such a fine book?' Duncan picked up Peazle's journal. 'It looks expensive. I see you've an expensive quill pen too.'

'I stole them from one of the bookstalls in Blair Street,' the pickpocket said. 'I always wanted to write something of value like men of learning do. Taught myself to read in the poorhouse, I did.'

'I cannae read nor write myself,' said the

highlander. 'Where I come from it was more important to learn how tae hunt and fight.' He lay down on the pile of rough sacks and straw that served as bedding in the Underground City. 'Still . . . it seems a shame to waste such a bonny book.'

'What do you mean?'

'Why don't you stop using it to dae the body-snatchers' dirty work? Keep a proper diary instead.' The highlander blew out the candle, plunging the vault into darkness. 'Someone might want tae read it years from now—then you'll live for ever.'

'I doubt that,' said the pickpocket. But he lay awake for a long time, smiling in the dark.

He had a proper friend at last and, to show his gratitude, he would take his new friend's advice.

The Giant

The next morning Charlie burst into the big top in a state of high excitement—Lily was balancing three chairs, one on top of the other, on the end of her chin.

'I read the diary! Last night! Well, some of it. It was amazing . . . just like I was there, in fact I don't even know if I dreamed it—' He stopped in mid-tirade. 'Isn't that a bit heavy?'

'Itsh jusht an illushion,' Lily said without taking her eyes off the chairs. 'You sheem very animated thish morning.'

'It's this diary. It was written by a boy called Peazle, a *real* boy from two hundred years ago! He had a best friend Duncan—he came down from the highlands to look for work in Edinburgh.' Charlie spread his arms, trying to convey the enormity of what he was saying. 'It wasn't like I was reading, it was like I was *seeing* what went on.'

'Musht be quite a book.'

'You don't understand. I can't explain it but somehow . . . I'm *not* just reading it. The book has only sketchy details and I only read a couple of pages, but I still know what went on in their lives.

Stuff that's not even written down.' Charlie pulled the diary from his rucksack. 'Listen. I have to go to Greyfriars Graveyard.'

Lily jerked her head back and the chairs collapsed in perfect formation, stacking neatly as they landed. Charlie blinked.

'Why Greyfriars Graveyard?' she said sharply.

'Eh? I want to see where Peazle liked to hang out—he used to write on the grave of some guy called Allan Ramsay. Duncan liked it too because it had hawks, just like the highlands.'

'Hawks?' Lily scowled.

'Well, one hawk. White with black-tipped wings.' Charlie held up the book. 'You want to come?'

'No I don't.' The girl turned sharply away. 'I have to practise.'

'Are you all right?' Charlie said, but Lily had begun to juggle again—seven balls, then eight, then ten, so fast they were merely a blur. She did not turn round as he left and he got the strangest feeling that the girl was suddenly upset and trying to hide it.

Greyfriars was only a few hundred yards from the Old Town but you could walk straight past without knowing it, for the cemetery was hidden by a high wall and still ringed by old buildings—Charlie was lucky to spot the entrance, set back from the street between a pub and a row of small shops. He let out a gasp as he walked through the wrought-iron gates. Dotted between the trees were lovingly carved gravestones, now weathered with age and, behind that, a high backdrop of grey Georgian tenements— exactly as he had seen them the night before! The boy walked round the side of the squat, barn-like church that faced the gates. There was the flat tombstone that marked the final resting place of Allan Ramsay, right where he knew it would be.

'This is more than a little weird,' Charlie muttered to himself, taking the journal from his bag. The flat worn stone was warm from the summer sun and, on impulse, he lay down on it—looking around to see if anyone disapproved. But the graveyard, hidden behind its double barricade, seemed to be deserted, so Charlie opened the book and began to read.

Sunday is the only day when Duncan duz not wurk at the factory and so we arranged to mete on the High Street in the afternoon, for in the morning he was paying his respects to a gypsy girl who sings for mony in Blair Street and with whom he is much taken. I was in powerful good spirits for I had releeved more than one rich merchant of his gold snufbox that week . . .

*   *   *

Peazle walked slowly down the High Street looking out for Duncan. Like all thoroughfares in the Old Town, the High Street was packed with people strolling and gossiping and it smelt strongly of sewage—for the ground was not paved and waste and rubbish was often thrown out of the windows at night. The air was filled with the shouts of fruit sellers and fishwives plying their wares from rickety wooden stalls planted in the stagnant mud. He finally found Duncan sitting on a stone stoop and looking glum.

'I presume things did not go entirely well with your girl this morning?' Peazle hunkered down beside his friend and tried to look sympathetic.

'She's no my girl, just a pretty lassie whose company I like.' Duncan poked dejectedly in the mud with his foot. 'I'm fond of her and she can sing love ballads fit tae break a heart but I'm a plain-spoken lad and not much for romantic talk.'

'Well, don't ask me for advice, I'm too scrawny for courting. You fancy a bag of buckies?' Peazle pointed to a stall selling little saucers of cockles covered in salt and pepper.

'I dinnae want to eat anything that looks like it came out of someone's nose,' the highlander grunted. Peazle bought a saucer anyway. He had taken to hanging around Edinburgh's bookstalls to hear what the learned gentlemen who browsed there were saying—usually he didn't understand a word but he could grab a silk handkerchief or gold coin from their back pockets as they strolled past. Last week the pickpocket had overheard one gent say that eating fish made people smarter and decided seafood was his best bet for getting an education. Since cockles were the only kind of marine life he could actually afford, Peazle had taken to eating them whenever he got the chance.

The two boys sat on the cracked step while Peazle shovelled cold, slimy shellfish into his mouth and Duncan glowered at the bronging crowds. The highlander badly missed the solitude of his heather-covered moors. Here he could see only slivers of sky between the tenement blocks and even those thin patches were tainted by thick palls of chimney smoke.

Duncan would have liked to get out of the grimy, overcrowded city for the day but Peazle insisted he was scared of the countryside. The pickpocket had lived his whole life in the slums and wasn't about to venture into a wilderness where they might both get eaten by a wild animal. Especially a camel. Peazle was deathly afraid of camels.

'There's nae camels in the Scottish countryside. I'm sure of it,' Duncan muttered.

'Have you ever seen a camel?' Peazle asked.

'I dinnae even ken what a camel is.'

'There you go then,' said Peazle triumphantly. 'The countryside could be full of man-eating camels and you wouldn't know it.'

Duncan wasn't giving up.

'We could go and climb up Arthur's Seat.' The highlander pointed south to where a craggy hilltop could be glimpsed through the swirling smoke and chimney pots. 'That's no exactly the countryside now, is it? You can see it from here.'

Peazle looked at his friend in horror.

'You must be joking! When that thing blows up I don't want to be standing on top of it.'

Idling outside his favourite bookstall the week before, Peazle had been horrified to hear two learned gents talking about Arthur's Seat being an extinct volcano with a vast network of tunnels underneath. Once he had asked around and found out what a volcano was, Peazle vowed never to set foot on the hill again. He was still trying to find out what extinct meant.

He half-heartedly offered the highlander a cockle but Duncan waved it away with a snort. Peazle could see his friend was in a foul mood but he wasn't about to go climbing over a volcano just to cheer him up. Duncan sighed loudly.

'Tell you what,' the pickpocket said finally. 'I'll

buy us some decent food for tonight, eh? I've had a good week and it's time to sell what I've . . . eh . . . acquired.' He wiped his greasy hands down his trousers and inspected his nimble fingers with pride. 'It means we'll have to go back to the Underground City for a bit, if you don't mind.'

'If I'm getting something other than boiled turnip for supper, I'm willing tae trek through the very gates of hell.'

'Funny you should say that.' Peazle grinned awkwardly as he stood. 'C'mon, let's get this over with.'

Duncan's mood was black as they marched back to the shadows of the South Bridge, stepped out of the sunlight and entered the familiar dark corridor that led to their vault. This time, however, the boys continued past the rude dwelling and carried on down the passageway. The highlander had never been in this direction before—he spent as much time as he could on the surface and had no inclination to delve deeper into the black smelly corridors.

'Never thought we'd end up back in here on my day off,' he muttered, tripping over a sleeping figure curled up on the tunnel floor. The passages, like every other part of Edinburgh, were festooned with down-and-outs who slept when they felt like it—and why not? In the permanent darkness of the Underground City it was always night.

'Here we are,' Peazle whispered finally, crouching beside a damp wall. 'There's a set of stairs behind a little opening down here—most people don't even know it exists.' His hunched form moved forward and, without warning, he was gone. Puzzled, Duncan shuffled one near-invisible foot around in front of him where the wall met the floor and felt a small opening—he could have passed it a hundred times in the blackness without realizing it was there. He sat down, wriggled his body through the gap and, leaning carefully on the slimy wall, inched slowly down a hidden stairway, feeling for each new step with his foot.

There was another tunnel at the bottom of the stairway and it seemed even darker than the one he had left, though Duncan didn't suppose this was actually possible. He heard a scratching noise to his right and Peazle's triumphant expression was lit by a crackling flame.

'Torches,' the pickpocket said proudly, waving a stout stick that dripped flaming tar in alarming amounts. 'Made 'em myself—you never know when the Old Town Guard will raid the place and I might have to make a quick getaway.'

Duncan sighed. Edinburgh's Old Town Guard were mostly ex-soldiers well over retirement age. It was unlikely that they would bother raiding a den of vice like the Underground City and weren't likely to catch more than a cold if they did.

In the light of the firebrand the highlander could see the stonework in this area was much older and cruder than the tunnels above and the walls shone with waterlogged moss. The smell was different, too; not the stink of stale sweat and smoke that filled most of the chambers, but a wet, earthy smell that reminded Duncan of the caves underneath highland waterfalls. Peazle moved away again and Duncan followed, touching the walls and sniffing his fingers.

'This is no bad, actually!' he grinned. 'Peaceful, ye ken? I canna hear anyone. Why does nobody live down here?'

'It's too damp and cold, even for beggars and drunks,' Peazle said. 'As far as I know there's only one person staying on this whole level and that's who we're going to see.'

'Who might that be?'

'His name's Shadowjack Henry, a blacksmith by trade—he moved down here a couple of months ago. There's a well at the end of this level that's been blocked up for as long as anyone can remember, so Shadowjack set up a wee forge and opened the well to draw water for it—he makes metal trinkets and sells them to the market traders on the High Street. The forge makes the vault warm enough to live in and there's no one else down here to pay rent to—a nice wee set-up, if you ask me.'

'Sounds like it,' Duncan agreed. 'How is it that I've never heard anyone mention him before?'

'You know how superstitious ignorant people are,' said Peazle, as if he had had the benefit of an Oxford education. 'There's some old legend about the well being haunted,' he continued with a laugh. 'Something about it leading straight down to hell.'

Duncan stopped. 'Let's go back.'

Peazle turned in astonishment.

'Eh? What's the matter?'

'I'm not going intae any haunted place,' said Duncan matter-of-factly.

'What?' Peazle spluttered. 'I thought highlanders weren't scared of man nor beast! At least, that's what you keep telling me about fifty times a day.'

'Haunted stuff isnae man nor beast.' Duncan

shook his head. 'Haunted stuff is witchies and kelpies and the Little People. In the Highlands you dinnae mess wi' creatures like that, especially the Little People.' He folded his arms in determination. 'I canna believe that you of all people would come down here, you that's scared of anything that moves.'

'I'm scared of camels and volcanoes but that's scientific stuff,' Peazle explained. 'This is the nineteenth century, Duncan. There's no such thing as Little People.' He sniffed. 'Most of the trouble we get is from big people.'

Duncan shook his head in exasperation but he was fiercely loyal to his friend and, after a stream of disapproving grunts, he finally indicated to keep going.

For a while the two boys walked without talking—the only sound being Peazle's tatty old boots crunching on loose stones and the rasp of his breathing. The pickpocket had to keep stopping to catch his breath, for a lifetime of sleeping in the Underground City and a diet of turnip and salted beef hadn't done much for his health. Duncan didn't try to hurry him, for the wiry highlander was concerned about his frail friend and wasn't all that keen to get to where he was leading anyway. Unlike Peazle, Duncan moved silently, as he had learned to do while stalking deer—only now he walked without a sound in case something was creeping up on *him*.

Eventually a flickering glow appeared at the far end of the tunnel and they could hear a muffled clanging, like a bell, growing louder as they walked. Peazle stopped and gave a long whistle and the ringing stopped. After a few seconds they heard a similar whistle coming from the direction of the light and Peazle signalled to Duncan that they could carry on. At the end of the passageway the boys turned a corner and a blast of hot, smoke-filled air seared their faces. They stepped from the dark passageway into a bright chamber and came upon a sight that would have confirmed the worst fears of the other underground dwellers.

Shadowjack Henry stood in the middle of the red, shimmering vault—stripped to the waist and swinging a huge hammer. He was so large that he made Merry Andrew look like a midget and his massive torso, shining with exertion, bore the livid weals of a hundred healed burns. He brought the hammer down on the glowing metal rod he was shaping and a shower of dazzling sparks flew into the air, vanishing into the fierce radiance that emanated from the blacksmith's forge. Over the fire a large metal smelting dish was suspended on a pole between two wooden tripods, powerful flames licking its sooty sides.

'My God,' whispered Duncan. 'We're in the doorway tae Hades itself.'

Shadowjack looked round. Huge teeth split his bushy black beard as he grinned at the pickpocket.

'Peazle, my lad.' He dropped the hammer with a clang and raised a sweaty hand in greeting. The smile vanished as he caught sight of Duncan. 'Ah. I see you brought a visitor.' Shadowjack Henry flexed his considerable muscles and two bushy eyebrows closed ranks on his sweaty forehead. 'I don't get many visitors,' he said coldly. 'Being a private sort of person.'

'This is Duncan MacPhail,' said the pickpocket, pointing to the highlander. 'Don't worry, he's a good friend and one that I would trust with my life.'

'That's the type of friend that you want, right enough,' said the giant smith, looking the highlander up and down before turning back to Peazle. 'So, what have you brought for me, my little man?' he said, suddenly brusque and businesslike.

The pickpocket pulled a canvas bag from under his shirt and emptied the contents onto the vault floor. Four snuffboxes glinted in the iridescent light. Shadowjack knelt down and inspected them.

'Solid gold and good quality too—they'll make a pretty puddle once they're melted down—well done, lad.' He went to a pile of bedding in the corner of the vault and rummaged inside. 'I'll give four shillings for the lot as I'm in an *uncommon* generous mood.' The blacksmith smiled broadly and folded a few coins into Peazle's hand, his massive fingers enveloping the boy's like a shark swallowing a minnow. Shadowjack cast a sideways look at Duncan to see if he had any opinion on the price but the highlander was staring into the well. It looked harmless enough, just a round hole in the corner of the vault floor with yet another wooden frame and pulley built over it. A stout rope and bucket sat nearby.

'Is this where you draw the water tae work your forge?'

'It is, boy.' The blacksmith nodded. 'And there are those who would like nothing better than for me to block that hole up again, but I'm far too big to argue with.' He motioned with his hand. 'Don't fall in, though, for I won't venture down to rescue you.'

'Don't worry, we're just going.' Peazle was wafting the air in vain, his face already running with sweat. 'Let's get out of here, Duncan, before I faint dead away with the heat.' The highlander was still trying to peer into the darkness of the well and Peazle grasped his arm and ushered him quickly out of the vault. Shadowjack didn't bother to say goodbye.

'He doesn't much like company, especially strangers,' the pickpocket said, as the red glow faded away behind them. He showed Duncan the pile of shillings. 'But I told you we'd eat well tonight.'

'That well back there.' Duncan paused. 'You can hear water running at the bottom.'

'So what?'

'Water in a well doesnae run anywhere—what I heard was a stream.'

'And that means?' Peazle looked none the wiser.

'I thought you were the scientific one,' the highlander scoffed. 'It means the water down there is coming from somewhere and going somewhere.'

He patted Peazle on the shoulder.

'It means there's another level underneath this one.'

*   *   *

Charlie sat up with a start, not sure if he had been dreaming or simply lost in his own thoughts. The sun had gone behind a cloud and Allan Ramsay's tombstone, wrapped in afternoon shadows, was now cold against his skin. He sat up quickly and closed the journal.

Charlie knew exactly where Shadowjack Henry had once worked, for he had been in that very chamber the day before and seen the remains of the blacksmith's forge—he recalled the discarded tripod and the stone circle. The pile of stones he had

removed must have been covering up the well—
sealed by some kind of iron plug—and just as well,
for hadn't the terrifying drumming noise come from
somewhere underneath it? Charlie shivered again and
he didn't think the sensation had much to do with
the temperature this time. All the same he looked up
to see where the sun had gone and his shiver turned
into a gasp.

Floating far above his head was a white hawk with
black-tipped wings.

The Dungeons

Charlie hurried back to the guest house, his mind in a whirl. Like the last time he had opened Peazle's diary, the boy was not sure if he had imagined or actually witnessed the events in the past. But there was no doubt that he had actually *seen* a hawk, right here and now, identical to the one Duncan described two centuries ago. Perhaps the bird's descendants still nested in the area and, by some genetic fluke, some bore the same markings. Then again, maybe *all* the hawks round here were white with black-tipped wings—Duncan didn't seem to know much about the lowland wildlife of Scotland and neither did Charlie.

Anyway, the boy had more pressing questions. How had Shadowjack Henry's well come to be blocked up again—hidden under a pile of rocks along with Peazle's book? What was the mysterious rapping he had heard in the Underground City? And what exactly happened to the boys from the past?

By the time Charlie reached the guest house his parents had left for their nightly performance at the big top. A little tray of biscuits and teabags were provided in each room, so the boy grabbed a handful

54

of chocolate digestives, opened the journal, and lay down on the bed to read.

The next Sunday we arranged to mete in the afternoon once more as Duncan had gone calling on his lady frend again and he seems to be a creeture of habit. I was bored wating and knowing that the castle esplanade was filed with gentlemen taking the air, I vowed to liten a few of their back pokets before returning to find my frend . . .

*   *   *

Edinburgh Castle was on the highest pinnacle of the Old Town ridge. The muddy road that led to it was steep and slippery and Peazle was wheezing like a donkey long before he reached the top. Eventually the slope opened onto the castle esplanade—an exposed area leading to the huge iron portcullis that fronted the massive fortress. Since the other three sides of the castle overlooked sheer cliff faces, the esplanade was the only real way to reach the castle— which left potential invaders horribly exposed. It was said that the approach was exactly the length an arrow could be accurately fired.

In peacetime, however, the esplanade's tremendous height made it the perfect spot for sightseeing and now the area was filled with young men trying to impress their lady friends by wearing their Sunday best and pretending to know the names of far off hills. Peazle strolled around like the city's scruffiest tourist, secretly eyeing young men buying cups of flavoured ice for their paramours and watching where they kept their purses.

'A fool and his money are soon parted—and love makes a fool of the wisest man,' the pickpocket said sagely. 'Ooh. I must write that down.'

While Peazle was spying on potential victims, Duncan sat at the bottom of Blair Street listening to the gypsy girl as she sang to the crowds. Like so many of the Old Town's narrow wynds, Blair Street sloped steeply down from the High Street until it vanished into the slums of the Cowgate at the bottom. Each wynd had its own distinct character and this particular thoroughfare was lined with bookstalls and filled with what Peazle always referred to as 'learned gents', browsing idly among the leather-bound volumes. Near the bottom of the wynd the stalls thinned out and there gents often paused to listen to the gypsy girl—for she had a voice that seemed to make words sweeter than any book could.

This time, however, her tune was making Duncan melancholy—a lament about the clans forced to leave their homeland after the doomed highland revolt of 1745. Even the girl's name reminded him of the highlands—Heather. Halfway through her refrain, Heather noticed Duncan's expression and broke off in mid-tune. She picked up a few grubby coins and, to the disappointment of the gathered gents, she came and sat beside him, her thick black hair swinging across her face as she lowered herself down.

'Is my singing making you sad?' she said, looking sideways at him.

'The song is,' he replied. 'And all the more for being sung so beautifully.'

'If you miss the highlands so much, why did you leave?' Heather asked. 'If I might be so bold,' she added quickly—for she knew the highlander wasn't one to reveal his feelings casually. But Duncan answered without any prompting, for the song had also reminded him of a great injustice—and he felt that injustices should always be brought into the open.

'The land my clan had worked for generations was taken from them so the laird could use it for his sheep to graze,' he said, with undisguised disgust. 'There was nae work any more for the men who lived there.'

'I'm sorry,' said Heather, but Duncan hadn't finished.

'An outbreak of cholera five years ago killed many, my own faither included. The rest of my clan booked passage tae North Carolina tae start a new life in the Americas.' The highlander's face was expressionless. 'My mother would not go.'

'Why not?'

There was a long silence before the boy spoke again.

'I had a brother, little more than an infant. Ma used to leave him in the doorway of oor croft wrapped in a wee tartan shawl while she picked wild berries—I was supposed to be watching him—I looked away for only a few seconds, I swear.' He kept his head bowed but the gypsy could hear the pain cracking his voice. 'When I turned back he was gone.'

Heather covered her mouth with her hand.

'I thought it must be a wolf or a starving dog that took him and I searched the moorland for days, but it was nae use.' Duncan's voice had suddenly grown hard and flat. 'Ma would not accept that. She said my brother had been taken by the Little People.'

'The fairy folk?' Heather nodded, unsurprised. In those days, people still believed in such creatures.

'Aye. My mother died herself of the cholera some months after but, until that time, she stood in the doorway every day at dusk and called my brother's name, hoping the Little People might take pity on her and bring him back.'

He looked up and smiled forlornly.

'They never did.'

Pretending to stare at the view, Peazle stretched out his hand and slowly lifted the tailcoat of the young man to his left, who was chatting animatedly to his lady. A stiff breeze blew from the Pentland Hills across the esplanade and tore at the youth's clothes, making the pickpockets practised manoeuvre impossible to detect. The wallet slid out of the back pocket, vanished into Peazle's vest and the pickpocket gave a satisfied smile—the young man was so engrossed in his belle that Peazle could have stolen his underwear. As the boy turned to escape, the grin froze on his lips.

Two kilted soldiers stood behind him pointing their bayonets at his stomach.

Heather sat silently beside Duncan and, for a while, she allowed the highlander his own thoughts. Eventually, however, she spoke again.

'Do *you* think the Little People took your brother?'

'I dinnae ken.' The highlander sighed. 'At our clan gatherings the old men used tae scare us with stories about them.'

'It was the same with us gypsies,' Heather agreed.

'According to our elders the Little People had many names—elves, faeries, sprites, imps, pixies, brownies—our legends say that they used to live all over the world. But as men began to spread across the globe so the Little People returned to their homeland of Galhadria.' The girl lowered her voice, as if some unseen being might be listening. 'They say that, in the quiet places of the earth, the Galhadrians sometimes return to dance or hunt and it is a great misfortune for any man to come upon them.'

Duncan was familiar with this part of the story. Children in the highlands had long been warned of 'thin places'—remote valleys and hilltops where the barrier between this world and the domain of the Little People was closest—though he had never heard the name Galhadria before. In these thin places, you might accidentally stumble on the Little People dancing in the moonlight and, if you did, they would take you to their world, against your wish. It wasn't that the Little People were evil, the old ones of the clan would say—it was just that the wishes of men didn't mean that much to them. Duncan supposed that was why they could take a human baby without worrying what it might do to a mother or brother.

'We were told that the Little People sometimes take our children and leave one of their own in its place,' he said. 'And you cannae tell it's really one of the fairy folk until it grows up. Or sometimes they leave a horrible deformed changeling. Or they dinnae leave anything at all. I wish I knew what was true.' He looked round at Heather. 'What's the matter?'

The gypsy girl was looking at the ground, her fists clenched.

'Nothing,' she answered quietly. 'I just think that legends can get mixed up over time. Even a small mix-up can change the meaning of everything, you know.' Heather paused, as if she had more to say but, before Duncan could press her, she scrambled to her feet.

'I'd better give them another song. Something more cheerful.' She smiled and nodded towards another group of wealthy gentlemen milling around the nearest bookstall. She began to sing again and the men gathered round and reached into their pockets.

Peazle had never been inside the castle before and, though he was truly impressed by the lofty battlements and smoke-blackened towers, he wished at that moment he could be anywhere else on the planet. The two soldiers marched him up the winding cobbled road into the very heart of the fortifications, past endless stone barracks, cannons, and cooking fires. The castle hadn't seen a battle for half a century but it was still a military garrison and kilted recruits and officers in bright tartan trews and scarlet jackets stared as the pickpocket was escorted past. The air pulsed with the smell of roasting meat and the sound of shouted orders.

'What are you going to do with me?' he asked one of the soldiers timidly.

'If it were oop ter me, lad, oi'd probably joost shoot yer,' he replied in a thick Irish brogue. 'Boot it's ter the doonguns oim taking yer.'

'The dungeons!' Peazle squealed, then quickly regained his composure. Panicking wasn't going to help this situation. 'I thought they were only for prisoners of war.'

'Dat dey are,' the soldier replied. 'Boot we're not at war with anyone at present and as it happens there's a coople o' men down dere from the town council—so I reckon oil joost hand yis over to them.' He motioned with his bayonet towards an oak doorway set in a tower wall and the other soldier pushed Peazle through. Behind the door a steep staircase wound into the bowels of the castle and the soldiers' tackety boots clattered on the stone as they followed Peazle round and round and down and down, past cold gaping chambers fortified with iron bars. In the darkness of some of the vaults Peazle could hear murmuring in some language he didn't understand.

'Dootch smooglers,' said the talkative Irishman. 'Oi can't oondershtand a bloody werd they're saying.'

The trio eventually arrived at a long corridor lit by thick, acrid candles. A group of men, two soldiers and two civilians, were clustered round a table cluttered with paper, trying to read in the flickering light.

'Sah! The tunnel don't show up on any of the charts we have!' a soldier with a giant walrus moustache barked. The civilians gave a little jump. 'There's no telling where it might lead. Might be a few feet or . . . '

' . . . Or it might lead right under our defences, yes, sergeant.' The other soldier, an officer of some sort, folded his hands behind his back. 'We simply have to find out where it goes. Can't fit any of our men in there, you say?'

'No, sah!' The civilians winced again. 'Not even Private Hemmingway—an' he lost his legs at Waterloo.' The sergeant thought for a second before adding, 'And an arm.'

The officer sighed. The sergeant turned to Peazle and his guards. 'What are you doing with that boy, Private MacSorry?'

'Caught him stealing, sor. Wallets. Oop on the esplanade.'

'That's not a military matter, private,' said the officer, brusquely.

'I know, sor, and I tot since dere were two members of the town council here, oid bring him to dem.'

The councillors, dressed in identical breeches and frock coats, looked up from the charts. 'It's not our concern, soldier,' one said. 'Deliver him to the town guard. He'll most likely be tried by the magistrate on Monday.'

The officer stroked his moustache thoughtfully before speaking. 'What will happen to the boy?'

'It's a serious charge, pickpocketing, if he was caught red-handed.' The councillor went back to studying the charts. 'He'll be deported to a penal colony in Australia, like as not.'

Peazle raised his hand. 'Actually, I was just testing these fine soldiers' powers of observation and very alert they were too. I was going to put the money back . . . '

'Don't even bother, lad.' The officer crouched down beside Peazle and put a hand on his shoulder. 'But there *might* be a way we could forget this whole . . . ehm . . . incident.'

'Oh, I don't think that's possible.' The councillor looked up again. 'Boy broke the law.'

'What I'm proposing, lad,' the officer ignored the interruption, 'is for you to redeem yourself by a bit of bravery. Like a little soldier, eh?' Peazle nodded enthusiastically, not having a clue what the officer was talking about. Encouraged, the man continued.

'We've found a tunnel in the dungeons, lad, didn't even know it was there. And we need to know where it goes but it's too small for any of my men to fit in, see?'

Peazle nodded again, more slowly this time—he was beginning to understand what the officer was getting at.

'So if you was to have a little explore of this tunnel and tell us where it went, the army would consider this an act of patriotism—a great civic duty. Isn't that right, gentlemen?'

Now the councillors were nodding as well. Private MacSorry gave Peazle a thumbs up sign.

'True. A boy would be forgiven a bit of thievery if he was as patriotic as that,' one councillor said slyly. 'Wouldn't get sent to Australia neither.'

Peazle looked from one looming adult to another. They leaned towards him, moustaches bristling.

'All right,' said the pickpocket wearily. 'Show me the tunnel.'

'Wait a moment. How will we know where he's gone?' the other councillor spoke.

'Drum, sah!' screamed the sergeant and the councillors jumped again. 'There's a tiny drum in the officers' mess, it was made for Colonel Grouper's little boy—before he blew his head off playing with a loaded musket!'

'All right, sergeant. Fetch the drum and a

firebrand for the lad.' The officer leaned further towards Peazle. 'We're going to make a hero of you, son, rather than a villain,' he whispered, not unkindly.

* * *

Charlie sat up in bed covered in sweat. He was still fully dressed but his mother must have removed his shoes and put a cover over him when she came home. The curtains were open and he could see the moon shining behind the spires of Edinburgh.

'My God . . . the legend,' he whispered to himself, remembering the rapping he had heard in the Underground City.

'Peazle's the little drummer boy.'

The Descent

Charlie felt as if he had slept for hours, even though it was still dark, and perhaps he had, for now he was wide-awake and itching to get up and do something. He put on his shoes, stuffed the diary inside his shirt and went to the window. The Old Town was hunched in the middle of Edinburgh like a sleeping dragon, a heavy moon gilding its jagged outline. Charlie looked at his watch. It was four-thirty in the morning. He unlatched the window and stuck his head out—there was a drainpipe a couple of feet to the left but his room was on the second floor and it was too dark to tell whether the garden below was grass, soil, or paving. Yet suddenly he wanted to know. In fact, he wanted to know everything—and not just know everything but *feel* everything, too— that was the closest he could come to describing it. For the first time Charlie Wilson really wanted to be part of the adventure rather than just a spectator.

Almost without thinking he pulled himself onto the broad window ledge and twisted round to grasp the drainpipe in both hands. He had never actually watched his parents practise their high-wire act but he remembered how they moved in the routines he *had* seen—and he recalled his father saying that hesitation was an acrobat's worst enemy. With a deep breath Charlie swung one foot over the pipe and planted it against the wall, took his other foot off the windowsill and began to climb down, hand over hand. A minute later he was standing on the dark dewy grass, not even out of breath.

'That was better than a video game,' he said brightly, letting himself out of the garden gate, and heading towards the Old Town.

Edinburgh Festival's events went on until around one in the morning and the pubs closed even later, but at this hour even the most hardened partygoers had gone to bed and the streets were deserted as Charlie made his way up the High Street and onto the castle esplanade. Far below, the lights of Edinburgh glittered like a swarm of fireflies but the castle was a soaring block of darkness, casting a net of shadows over the esplanade and turning monuments and trees into sinister blobs. Charlie felt as if he was standing on another world.

Then the first rays of dawn began to filter through the tall tenements on the Royal Mile, spotting the castle ramparts with light and laying golden strips along the esplanade. They lit a low bordering wall and Charlie went and sat on the ground with his back against it. As the minutes ticked by the castle slowly turned from black to charcoal to grey and the boy could make out the outline of statues, railings, and ticket booths. Eventually it was light enough to read and he opened Peazle's diary.

The tunel was at the bak of the darkest deepest dungon and there was hardly room for even a boy of my small size to fit inside. I held the firebrand in front of me with one hand and dragged the drum behind me on a lether strap tied to my waste. The oficer had instructed me to stop every few minutes or so and bang the drum as loudly as I cood, so that he could hear where I was going, but this proved to be more difficult than he imagined . . .

*　　*　　*

The firebrand sputtered badly and the narrowness of the tunnel deflected the heat back into Peazle's face—he was forced to hold the torch as far in front of him as he could and crawl using his free arm. The leather strap attached to the drum kept getting tangled in his legs and the only way he could make a noise was to stop crawling and kick at the drum's taut skin with his feet.

The councilmen and soldiers at the entrance to the tunnel waited until the erratic banging was so faint they could hardly hear it.

'Sergeant,' the officer said finally, 'take some men and scour the main courtyard, see if they can pick up the noise there. Put some out on the esplanade too.'

'Yes, sah!' The sergeant stood to attention, then hesitated. 'Beggin' your pardon, sah, but that drum the lad's dragging behind him fills the entire tunnel. If it comes to a dead end how's he going to get back?'

'This is a military garrison.' The officer gave the sergeant a withering look. 'We can't just have tunnels running who knows where. We need to know where it goes.' Then he turned and walked away.

Wriggling along the tiny passageway Peazle was soon close to exhaustion—the firebrand in front of him was burning precious oxygen, what air he could suck into his straining lungs was hot and thin, and his elbows and knees throbbed where the rough stone had torn away the skin. Worst of all, he was gripped by a rising panic that was becoming harder and harder to quell—he wanted to scream in rage and fear and thrash at the walls but he knew that this would use up even more air. Instead he forced himself to lie still until he felt a semblance of calm return. Then he began to crawl forward once more.

Finally, when the pickpocket had almost given up hope, the little passage began to widen. Soon Peazle could crawl on his hands and knees, then manage a crouching shuffle and, finally, he was able to stand. He put the torch on the ground, fastened the drum properly round his waist and untied the drumsticks strapped to his thigh.

On the esplanade, Private MacSorry sat on a low wall smoking a pipe.

'MacSorry!' roared the sergeant. 'I know the boy's probably dead already or his extremities are being eaten by rats but that doesn't mean you can give up looking . . . ' He stopped suddenly and held up a large scarred hand. 'What's that?'

'What's what?'

'Silence, you horrible little man!' the sergeant screamed. 'How am I supposed to concentrate with you wittering on!' He dropped to his knees and pressed a hairy ear to the ground.

'That's drumming, private, that's what it is. Under the ground.' He looked up, moustache quivering, and beckoned to the officer. 'Sah! Over here!'

Peazle marched along the tunnel, firebrand raised high. Occasionally he stopped and beat the drum for a few seconds, but not very often for the sound was deafening in such an enclosed space. The boy was wary of making a loud noise at the best of times for pickpockets, out of sheer habit, didn't like to attract unwanted attention—and who knew what lurked in these passageways? But, however alarming the drumming was, Peazle was far more disconcerted by the fact that the tunnel had begun to slope steeply down. Now, with every step, he was moving deeper into the bowels of the earth.

Then he came to the door.

It was ancient and thick, its misshapen oak timbers covered in dark mould. Peazle groaned in disbelief.

'What on God's green earth is *this* doing here? It must weigh a ton and I'll wager its hinges are rusted solid with age.' He gave a half-hearted shove at the oak giant. 'I bet Goliath himself couldn't shift it.'

The door swung open without a sound and Peazle fell through into another passage. The barrier shut again and the pickpocket sprang to his feet, swiping wildly at the air with his drumsticks and screaming— but no hidden monster appeared and this tunnel looked the same as it did on the other side of the door. Regaining his composure, Peazle turned and inspected the barrier more closely. The torch lit up the hinges, ornate, finely crafted, and looking as if they had been made yesterday.

'No wonder they didn't rust,' the pickpocket breathed. 'If I'm not mistaken they're solid silver—

finer than any snuffbox I ever seen.' He ran his torch excitedly over the rest of the door—and found that its surface was pitted with metal studs, glowing with a flickering beauty. They too were silver. Peazle grabbed a narrow rock and tried with all his strength to prise one off, but the stud stayed put.

'Damn!' The pickpocket finally gave up. 'Don't suppose there's much chance of stumbling on a crowbar.' He stepped back and studied the door with a growing suspicion. 'Why would anyone go to the trouble of building such an ornate barricade way down here then make it so easy to get through?'

His eyes widened.

'Unless it only opens from one side!'

The pickpocket launched himself at the door and pushed with all his might. It didn't budge. He tried pulling on the silver studs but his hands just slipped off.

'Blast, blast, blast!!!' he sobbed, and attacked the door again, but he already knew in his heart that it was useless. He gave the unyielding wood one last kick, picked up the firebrand and continued, still cursing, down the tunnel. But the unpleasant surprises weren't over for, before long, the tunnel forked. Peazle stopped and stared at the identical passageways.

'Ach, both of these probably lead to certain death, so it doesn't matter which one I take,' he muttered, and went left. But after a while the tunnel split again and then again and every few minutes he had to make a fresh choice. Peazle tried to pick the passages that didn't slope too much—but each corridor twisted and turned and led inexorably downwards. Desperation eventually overcame fear and, as the boy marched, he began to beat the drum—berating himself with each stroke for agreeing to this insanity. He would probably keep descending until he died from thirst or ended up in Australia after all. Then he turned a corner and stopped dead.

Once again the passageway split in different directions but, this time, the left-hand passage opened into a large chamber. It seemed to have suffered a rock fall—on one side of the vault boulders rose at a steep angle from the floor almost to the roof.

The pickpocket's mouth fell open and the drumsticks fell unnoticed from his hands. Scattered across the sloping hill of stones was a mass of breastplates and helmets—while swords, spears, and arrows protruded from between the larger rocks. They glowed coldly in the firebrand's light and Peazle could tell at a glance that the weapons and armour, like the door studs, were made of solid silver.

The pickpocket was looking at more wealth than he could ever have imagined—and he could imagine a lot of wealth. He clambered onto the rock fall and ran trembling hands over the shining surfaces.

'This is the *best* thing that ever happened to me,' he sighed, laying his cheek reverently on a gleaming breastplate. 'Now I really do have to get out of here alive.'

He cast an expert eye over the treasure until he spotted what he was sure was the finest piece—near the ceiling a beautifully engraved sword with a jewel-encrusted handle was wedged between two boulders. The pickpocket scrambled to the top, grasped the handle and pulled with all his might. The sword slid out of the narrow gap—astonishingly light in his hand and smouldering with a steely blush that seemed to come from within.

'This one will do nicely.' Peazle climbed back down the rock pile, the drum banging awkwardly against his knees. With a grunt he unfastened a clasp on the leather strap and the drum crashed to the ground and rolled off down the tunnel. Peazle fastened the sword in its place, picked up the firebrand and set off down the open passage whistling to himself. Now that he carried a weapon worth a fortune, the pickpocket was filled with a new-found enthusiasm.

Halfway down the Royal Mile, the sergeant took his ear from the ground and slowly stood up. On one side of his head his hair, matted with mud, stuck out like a small explosion. The councillors and the officer looked at him expectantly.

'The drumming kept getting fainter, sah, like the boy was getting further and further underground.' The sergeant took a deep breath. 'Then it stopped.'

There was silence for a few seconds before the officer turned to the councillors.

'I doubt very much if we've found an escape tunnel or a secret entrance to the castle—not if it goes down that far.' He turned to the sergeant. 'Just to be on the safe side, order the men back to the dungeons and have them seal the passage up again.'

'Ehm. Begging pardon, sah.' The sergeant looked flustered, for he was not used to questioning his superiors. 'Just because the drum stopped doesn't mean the boy is dead.'

'No indeed, sergeant.' The officer tapped an ivory-topped cane angrily against his leg. 'But my priority is the defence of the castle, not the fate of some thief.' He quickly turned his back, indicating that their brief conversation was over.

'Yes, sah.' The sergeant motioned to MacSorry and his companions to follow and marched purposefully back up the High Street. He had seen children die before—the drummer boy of his own regiment had been swept away in a French cannon blast at the battle of Auerstadt. He didn't approve, of course, but orders were orders.

*   *   *

Charlie opened his eyes—the whole of the esplanade was bathed in early morning sunlight and the brass statues that lined the sides were shining like precious metal.

'Breastplates and helmets and swords,' the boy breathed softly. 'All solid silver and encrusted with jewels.' He remembered Lily's words when he had first shown her the note.

I bet it means there's treasure hidden down there . . .

'You said it, girl!' laughed Charlie, shutting the diary. Then the laugh died in his throat as he recalled what she had said next.

What if those council workers are heading towards it?

Charlie sprang to his feet and raced down the High Street towards the big top.

The Forge

Charlie half expected to see Lily juggling elephants or something equally bizarre when he burst into the theatre but she was sitting on the floor, in her usual green dress, drinking a can of Coke.

Charlie's face was red and sweating after running halfway down the Royal Mile so Lily held out the drink to him. He took a huge gulp and bubbles shot out of his nose.

'Charming.'

'Listen!' the boy spluttered after three minutes of uncontrollable hiccuping. 'There really is treasure in the Underground City—in a set of blocked-up tunnels! It's in Peazle's journal. Erm. Sorry.' He handed the can, overflowing with froth, back to Lily who looked at it in disgust. 'There's silver. Loads of it, according to this book.'

'Told you.' Lily allowed herself a triumphant little smile.

'Yeah, but we're in trouble. There's council workers excavating down there—you said so yourself.' Charlie pointed to the back of the big top. 'We need to get underground and find that treasure before they do.'

'We? I thought I was just the lookout.'

'I don't know about you,' said Charlie hotly, 'but that treasure would mean an awful lot to me. You've never seen where I live—it's small and cheap 'cause my parents hardly make any money. If you hadn't noticed, there isn't exactly a lot of work at the job centre for acrobats.'

'Hey, hey.' Lily held up a hand. 'Calm down. Take a seat.' She pulled Charlie down beside her and he sat, chest heaving—trying to get his emotions, as well as his breathing, under control.

'For a start you don't know if the council workers are digging anywhere near the treasure.'

'But they might be,' Charlie interrupted, running his hand through his hair. 'They might reach it any day.'

'Yes. But you don't *know* that.' Lily took the boy's hand and stared earnestly into his face, her green eyes somehow soothing him. 'Charlie, we don't even know if the treasure is still there.' The boy began to shake his head but she squeezed his hand tighter. 'The diary is almost two hundred years old, remember?'

He nodded sullenly.

'You need to read the rest of the book before you go rushing back into those tunnels.' She gave one last squeeze before letting go of his hand. 'You need to find out exactly what's down there.'

'Yeah, yeah. You're right.' Charlie stood up and went to the ranks of chairs where the audience normally sat. He plonked himself down and pulled out the diary.

'What are you doing?'

'Taking your advice.' He looked up. 'I'm going

to finish the diary. Go ahead and juggle if you want.'

He went back to the book and began reading. Lily pulled several multicoloured balls from her pockets and began to toss them in the air, her hands moving faster and faster until they were no more than a pink smear. After a while the balls were joined by glittering stars, circling round each other like a tiny galaxy. One of the balls burst into flames without interrupting its mad spinning. Charlie didn't look up.

Lily sighed. The balls began to vanish one by one, their motions got slower, and the stars glittered less brightly and went out. Finally only the flaming ball spun uncertainly on the end of the girl's finger. With a flick of her wrist her hand enveloped the flame, snuffing it out, and the ball dropped, smoking, to the floor. Lily walked over to Charlie.

'Budge up then,' she said, sitting next to him. 'Let's have a look.'

The tunel seemed to be levelling out at last and I was no longer scared of meeting any monsters, or not very much, for I had my magnificent sword, which I intended to sell as soon as I could find my way to the surface . . .

*　　*　　*

'Uh oh.' Peazle looked up at his spluttering torch. The shadows in the tunnel were becoming thicker and darker as the firebrand's flame grew lower. The pickpocket increased his pace but he couldn't go much faster, for the extent of his ill health was making itself painfully obvious. The boy had a nagging stitch in his side, his breath was coming in ragged gasps, and the reduced light meant he stumbled on the uneven floor every few feet, sometimes sprawling head first across the pitted floor. On the fourth or fifth fall, he lay exhausted while the firebrand's flame faded to smoky embers and the tunnel melted into a terrifying blackness. Still lying on the floor, Peazle curled himself into a ball and began to cry.

But gradually his crying turned to a shivering whimper for the tunnel was cold and the heat Peazle had worked up during his earlier exertions was evaporating. He closed his eyes and pulled his elbows and knees in tighter, trying to shut out the cold and the darkness and the fear, but lying perfectly still made him aware of something he hadn't noticed before—he could hear a faint, sinister hiss somewhere up ahead.

'Snake?'

Peazle's eyes shot open and his hand went to the hilt of his sword—he drew the weapon slowly from his leather belt and held it protectively in front of his face. To his astonishment the sword glowed with a pale blue luminance—not as effective as the firebrand, but enough to let him see a few feet of the passage ahead. Peazle knew that lying doing nothing, no matter how scared he felt, wasn't going to help solve his predicament—and *something* was making that hiss. Of course it might be a giant underground snake, but then again it might be a wind blowing in from somewhere outside. There was only one way to find out, so he struggled to his feet and started forwards, jabbing the sword aggressively before him. Whenever the tunnel branched Peazle listened carefully then went in the direction of the noise— and he knew he was choosing well for, at each fork, the sound got louder—though never as loud as the pounding of his heart.

Then the passage ended and Peazle found himself looking into a smooth volcanic chamber, triangular in shape and not much higher than his head. At the narrow end a stream emerged from a rock fissure and rolled sluggishly through a gash in the floor eroded by centuries of flowing water. At the wider end it vanished into the darkness again. Peazle gripped his sword handle tighter, for the surface of the stream danced and sparkled with a strange red light that made the water look suspiciously like blood. The pickpocket had once overheard a conversation between two learned gents about Greek mythology, whatever that was. They recounted a story about how dead souls were ferried down an underground river and into Hell, which was guarded by a three-headed hound called Cerberus.

The pickpocket looked around in terror. 'Nice doggy,' he hissed and sank to his knees, clasping his hands in front of his face. 'Please please, get me out of this.' He closed his eyes, praying to whatever deity happened to be listening. 'I've always wanted to die rich, but not ten minutes after I *got* rich.' He opened one eye and looked pleadingly upwards. 'C'mon, I'll do anything. Just give me a sign.'

An object came hurtling out of the blackness above and plunged into the stream, showering the pickpocket with icy needles of water. He scuttled back against the chamber wall, gasping with cold and fear and waving his sword ineffectively in the general direction of the unknown attacker. The water broke again and a wooden bucket, tied to the end of a rope, emerged full and dripping from the watercourse. It rose jerkily back up and vanished into a red glowing hole in the chamber roof.

'Whoa! Hey! Whoever's up there!' the pickpocket screamed at the top of his voice. 'I'm down here! Here! Oh damn!'

He still held the silver sword. The pickpocket looked round in panic and, spotting a large boulder, ran over and pushed the sword into the shadows behind it. He whirled back, took a deep breath, jumped into the icy stream and waded to the centre of the chamber. Above him he could now see a long, thin funnel rising forty feet through the solid rock of the chamber roof and ending in a circle of red light. Suddenly he realized exactly where he was.

'Shadowjack! Shadowjack Henry! I'm down here!' the pickpocket yelled up the funnel. 'I'm down here!' He waved his arms maniacally, though nobody above could possibly see him. 'I'm at the bottom of your well!'

A bearded face appeared in the red circle far above.

'Peazle? Is that you I can hear, lad?' Shadowjack's voice echoed down the shaft. 'How the hell did you get down there?'

The rope and bucket came hurtling down again. Shivering and crying, Peazle sat on the bucket, arms and legs wrapped round the sodden rope and Shadowjack Henry pulled him to safety.

A few minutes later Peazle was sitting in Shadowjack's vault, wrapped in a woollen blanket and sipping a cup of hot ale. A pot of the sweet smelling brew bubbled on the forge and the pickpocket's clothes hung, steaming, on the bar above. Shadowjack sat next to the boy, stripped to the waist, holding his own mug in a giant scarred hand. He listened intently, nodding occasionally, while Peazle told him about his underground journey. The pickpocket missed out the part about the treasure—he wasn't about to trust such a big man with so much wealth at stake.

'That's a fine adventure without a doubt,' he said when Peazle had finished. The two stared at each other for a long time, until the blacksmith spoke again.

'If you go back to the surface they'll probably just arrest you.'

Peazle nodded bitterly.

'No. I don't think I'd be much of a friend if I let you go back to the surface.' Shadowjack stroked his beard slowly, still looking keenly at the boy. The pickpocket couldn't see much friendliness in that stare.

They sat in silence for a while longer, Shadowjack still staring intently. Finally Peazle couldn't stand it any more.

'You know about the treasure, don't you?' he said bluntly.

'Aye, I do,' Shadowjack admitted. 'You think anything but treasure would keep me in this hellhole? I've not seen a bloody tree in three months.'

The giant stretched a burly arm over the forge and shifted Peazle's clothes so they wouldn't scorch. He took another gulp of his ale.

'I was a fine smith, you know,' he said, after a long pause. 'Working out by Kelty across the River Forth. I did all right when we was fighting Napoleon and the army needed cannon and cartwheels and the like. But after the war, many that harvested the land left for the cities for they have machines now that can do their work.' Shadowjack spat on the floor to show what he thought of mechanized farming. 'Me? I couldn't work in some hot, sweaty, cramped factory.'

Peazle looked incredulously around the sweltering little vault. 'Then how on earth did you end up down here?'

'I went to Leith docks to enlist in the King's Navy—I'd got to quite like cannon. Thought I might make a good cabin boy.'

Peazle frowned. He could never tell if Shadowjack was joking or just slightly insane. The big man carried on with his tale of woe regardless.

'I was having a last whisky or three in one of the taverns there when I overheard two gypsy types talking in a corner—a mite the worse for the grog they were, and a bit louder than they intended to be. I only caught the end of what they were saying—but it sounded powerful interesting to me. Another ale?'

'No thanks.'

Shadowjack poured more steaming liquid into the boy's cup anyway.

'One was telling the other some old gypsy legend— about how there was supposed to be treasure hidden in a well under Edinburgh.' Shadowjack took another large swig of his ale—the fact that it was still boiling didn't seem to bother him. 'And he'd heard from a beggar that there happened to be a blocked-up well at the bottom of the Underground City.'

'So you decided to abandon a life on the ocean wave and move *here*?' Peazle looked sceptical.

'Well, to be honest, I can't swim.' The big

blacksmith took a deep breath. 'Besides, the only ship in port was a barge carrying treacle to Glasgow. So I came down here, built a forge and opened up the well.' He pointed to the forbidding hole in the corner of the vault. 'Late at night I'd climb down the shaft and search for the treasure. Took me a while to find it—not as fast as you, eh?'

'Yes. I was born lucky.' Peazle snorted. Then he had a thought. 'How are you going to get all that treasure out without anyone spotting it?'

'Simple. I'm melting it down in the forge.'

'You're what!'

Instead of replying Shadowjack padded over to the darkest corner of the vault and picked up a large knife. Peazle clutched his mug tighter but the blacksmith pulled a horseshoe from his pocket, scraped at it with the blade and held it out. Under the dirty iron surface the metal gleamed brightly. Peazle drew in breath sharply.

'Throw on a bit of dirt when it's hot and a silver horseshoe will look as drab and worthless as any iron one. When I've turned all the treasure into these horseshoes, I'll pile them on a cart and ride out of Edinburgh a rich man. Your outfit's dry.'

Warily, Peazle took the stiff, warm clothes and began to put them on. Shadowjack stood up and stretched—the movement put him between the pickpocket and the vault door and his shadow rose menacingly up the wall and flickered across the roof. He was still holding the knife.

'There's only one flaw in my plan.' He looked darkly at the boy and Peazle shrank back from the bushy gaze. 'If anyone told on me, I'd find myself fighting off every thief and beggar in the city.'

'*I* wouldn't tell,' Peazle said in a small voice. 'Not ever.'

'I want to believe that, lad,' said Shadowjack taking a step forward. Peazle saw that the giant was sweating more than he ever had working on his forge. The knife was still in his hand, reflecting the blood-red glow of the fire. 'I like you, boy, but that's an awful lot of treasure down there.'

Peazle began to back away as Shadowjack advanced. His mind was working furiously.

'You're right, that *is* an awful lot of treasure.' He saw to his horror that the blacksmith was herding him towards the mouth of the well. 'It can't be easy melting it down on your own.'

'True.' Shadowjack shifted the knife from one hand to the other, still moving towards the boy. 'I don't like to leave the vault for more than a few minutes in case someone stumbles on my little operation and that makes the job slow going.'

'How many horseshoes have you made in the last month?'

'Three.'

'I take your point.' Peazle was at the edge of the well-mouth now. He could hear the gurgle of the water below and feel cold air rising at his back.

'What if you had help!' he said quickly. 'You could be finished before you knew it.'

Shadowjack stopped and raised a thick black eyebrow. 'Help?'

'Suppose *I* was to go down the well and bring out the silver for you to smelt down. My friend Duncan could be a lookout—he's from the highlands—nobody can sneak up on him unawares and he's handy with a sword if they did.' Peazle struggled to keep the fear out of his voice and to sound as reasonable and businesslike as possible. 'Shadowjack, there's enough silver down there to make all three of us rich a dozen times over.'

The blacksmith tapped the knife against his cheek while Peazle teetered on the edge of the well.

'All right, lad,' he said suddenly. 'You have a deal.' He shot out a meaty paw and grasped Peazle's hand. The force of his handshake lifted the boy away from the menacing hole and he bounced around on the end of the blacksmith's arm like a rag doll.

'Shadowjack,' he said, through rattling teeth. 'Why didn't those gypsies come looking for the treasure themselves?'

The shaking stopped. 'I don't know, lad,' the giant blacksmith said evenly. 'Leith's a rough area. Maybe something . . . unfortunate happened to them.'

He let go of the pickpocket's hand and gave a toothy grin.

'Off ye go. Find your pal and come right back. Don't ask any more daft questions.'

And Peazle went, still shaking like a leaf.

The Gorrodin-Rath

Charlie shut Peazle's diary with a snap.

'Well, that's that, isn't it?' he snorted. 'They took the treasure and buggered off out of Edinburgh. I might have known we wouldn't be lucky enough to find it still down there.'

'Don't be so sure.' Lily tapped the dirty old book. 'If those guys rode into the sunset with the silver then why was Peazle's diary still in the Underground City?'

Charlie arched an eyebrow. 'If I had that much money a stupid diary would be the last thing on my mind.'

'Even if it implicated you in stealing a fortune?'

'Ah. I never thought of that.' Charlie pointed an appreciative finger at Lily and opened Peazle's diary again.

Duncan, Shadowjack, and myself began removing the silver. I wood take a piece of armor or a sword, carry it to the botom of the well and put it in the bucket and Shadowjack would haul it up, melt it down and beet it into a horseshoe shape. Duncan kept a lookout and fetched food and water and by this method, working day and night, we quickly transformed all the silver untill there were only a few pieces left . . .

* ★ ★

Duncan sat on a pile of rags in the doorway of the vault where he and Peazle lived. The chamber was one of the last in this particular tunnel and an ideal place to keep watch to see if anyone walked past, heading for the hidden staircase. The highlander didn't know why he was bothering—in the week they'd been working not one person had shown the slightest interest in going in the direction of the blacksmith's vault. The combination of superstition and an understandable fear of an antisocial giant like Shadowjack Henry had effectively dampened the curiosity of the Underground City dwellers. Even the likes of Merry Andrew stayed away.

Today was the last day of their enterprise—the armour and weapons were almost all gone and a huge pile of dirt-covered horseshoes was now piled in the corner of Shadowjack's chamber. The blacksmith had used all his savings to purchase a horse and cart, which was now tethered in stables at the Pleasance Meadows a few hundred yards away. At dusk the trio would transport the booty to the surface, load it onto the cart and drive it through the city gates, claiming it was a delivery for the cavalry at Ruthven Barracks. Once they were out of Edinburgh they would turn and head for Glasgow where crooked merchants would pay a fortune for such an amount of pure silver. And it certainly was pure—in fact it was the most beautiful material Duncan had ever seen.

Tomorrow he would be a rich man. In a few days, he and Peazle would take their share and he would have the money to buy a plot of land in the highlands—perhaps even enough to travel the world.

Yet he wasn't happy. Everything had to be done in secret, for how could three peasants like him, Peazle, and Shadowjack claim to have honestly come by such wealth? He would have to leave Edinburgh without telling anyone and adopt another identity to buy his farm—and he would never see Heather again. He could not bear to spend his life slaving in some Edinburgh factory but what was the use of having one's own land when you could not use your own name and when you had no family or loved ones to share your riches with?

And why shouldn't he take someone? In fact, why couldn't he take Heather? He had always felt he had nothing to offer such a beautiful and talented girl but now he would have enough money for both of them to live comfortably and surely she must be tired of singing for a living in these cramped and filthy streets? She claimed to be a gypsy, after all, so she must share his love of open skies and uncluttered spaces. He could take her away and look after her properly.

His mind made up, he hurried out of the Underground City to find Heather, leaving Shadowjack and Peazle working unawares in the darkness below.

Shadowjack put on thick leather gloves and grasped the sides of the giant smelting dish—it bubbled above the forge, hooked on a metal pole suspended between two wooden tripods. The blacksmith carefully tipped the container until a small amount of molten silver trickled into a curved stone mould on the vault floor. When it began to harden he plucked the silver from the mould with iron tongs and hammered it into a proper horseshoe. Sparks drifted through the air and singed the smith's beard—but he was used to this and paid it no heed. Like Duncan, he was deep in thought.

It was a shame to have to split all this lovely treasure with the boys. Then again, he had to admit Peazle and Duncan had worked hard and he certainly couldn't have pulled the job off without them. Besides, that boy Duncan was a tough character and Peazle certainly wasn't stupid.

Ach, it was only money, after all. He just needed enough to get to America, find some unclaimed land and open his own smithy there—for that was the work he loved. Shadowjack held up the finished horseshoe, swept it through a pile of soot and dirt and plunged it into the bucket of water causing a mighty blast of steam to rise into the air.

Peazle sat at the bottom of the rock pile trying to draw a proper lungful of air. In the last few days his breathing had become more and more laboured and now bouts of coughing racked his frail body. The boy's health was rapidly getting worse and he suspected he had consumption, but he had to keep going—until he had his share of the treasure he couldn't afford medical treatment. Thank goodness there were only a couple of pieces left. He struggled to his feet but another fit of coughing forced him back to his knees. He wiped the back of his hand across his trembling mouth and it came away smeared red. The pickpocket clenched his fists, gritted his bloody teeth, and forced himself to stand.

Still coughing he picked up a helmet and, with a breathless sob, staggered back into the tunnel.

Heather was singing at the bottom of Blair Street as she always seemed to be—it occurred to Duncan that, for a gypsy, she seemed remarkably fond of staying in one spot. She saw him as he came down the hill and quickly finished her song, waving goodbye to the clapping gents as she ran over. She gave Duncan a hug, standing on tiptoe to get her arms round his neck.

'Hey, stranger,' she said breathlessly. 'I haven't seen you all week.'

'Work, work, work, that's me,' the highlander replied solemnly. He motioned for the girl to sit beside him. 'Heather, I think we need tae talk.'

'I thought you were ignoring me.' Heather grinned and sat down. 'Why so serious? Oh. I forgot. You're always serious.'

The highlander smiled at the mild rebuke and took her hand. 'What would you dae if you had enough money to get out of Edinburgh?' he said.

'I don't. Have enough money, that is.'

'Suppose I got it.'

'I've lived too long in this city to make any wishes.'

'I might . . . be on tae something.' Duncan ran a hand through his long dark hair, unsure of how to finish. 'Something that will make me . . . well . . . awfy rich.'

'What are you talking about? Have you broken the law? Are you in trouble?'

'Oh, for goodness' sakes!' The highlander

thumped a hand on his knee. 'I've aye been a plain speaker—I dinnae ken any other way. Me and Peazle found treasure. A lot of treasure, at the bottom of the Underground City under an auld well. We've almost finished taking it out and it's enough to make us all . . . ' His voice trailed away. 'What's wrong?'

Heather's face had gone white. 'Treasure?' She put a trembling hand on the highlander's knee. 'At the bottom of a well?'

'Incredible, isn't it?'

'Is it silver? Weapons and armour made of silver?'

'Aye, silver.' The highlander's delight turned to puzzlement. 'Wait a minute. How did you ken that?'

'Duncan. I think we need to talk.'

Shadowjack saw the rope suspended over the well jerk several times, a sign that Peazle was pulling at the other end. He put down his tongs and walked over to the hole.

'How many more, lad?' he shouted down.

'I've tied a helmet to the rope. You can pull it up now.' Peazle's voice drifted up. He sounded exhausted. 'There's only a shield left but it's bigger than all the other pieces.' There was a fit of coughing from the darkness. 'I don't know that I can carry it, Shadowjack. It looks awful heavy.'

'Go back to the rock fall and have a rest, wee man,' Shadowjack shouted back. 'I'll melt the helmet then climb down and help you.'

'Will do.'

The helmet clanked back and forth against the sides of the shaft as the blacksmith pulled it up. When it reached the top, he leaned over the well

mouth and untied it from the rope. As he finished
unfastening the knot a blast of cold air hit him, rising
up from the black depths. Shadowjack shivered
violently and dropped the helmet, then peered into
the hole, bemused. He had been working in this
vault, hauling water and then bits of armour out of
the shaft, for three long months and he'd never felt
slightly cold before. Now, for some reason, the hairs
were standing up on the back of his neck and his
calloused skin was covered in goose bumps.

Peazle trudged back to the rock pile and lowered
himself onto the floor—it seemed chillier down here
than it had ever been before. He set his aching back
against a boulder, stretching and twisting to try and
relieve the pain in his tired muscles. He picked up a
little flask of whisky Shadowjack had given him and
took a sip.

'Whooooeeeegh. Eugh! Eugh! Eeeeeeeeeugh!' He
shuddered, putting it quickly down again. 'I can't
believe people drink this stuff for fun.' But he had to
admit Shadowjack's 'medicine' had warmed him a
little and, after a while, his neck bent and he closed
his eyes.

Suddenly there was a sharp noise to his left and
his head jerked up. A small stone tumbled down the
rock pile and landed a few feet away. Peazle sighed
in relief, unclenching his fists.

'I will be *so* happy when I get out of this place,'
he wheezed, sinking back. 'My imagination is starting
to get the better of me.'

But, for some reason he could not fathom, the
pickpocket did not dare close his eyes again.

'We gypsies know many legends, Duncan.' Heather looked the highlander straight in the eye. 'And to be honest, some are just make-believe. But others we don't take lightly.'

'It's the same in the highlands,' Duncan agreed. 'What of it?'

'There is a legend,' she continued in whispered tones, 'that I think you should hear about. According to the gypsies, many centuries ago one of the Little People was a great magician called Gorrodin—exiled from Galhadria for a reason I do not know. His heart was filled with bitterness and he decided that, if he could not live on his own land, he would set up a kingdom on earth.' Lily pointed to the hill always ominously present over Edinburgh's rooftops. 'In a great cavern under Arthur's Seat he created an army of goblins and trolls called the Gorrodin-Rath and favoured them with magic artefacts—including a cup that bestowed eternal life on anyone who drank from it. They terrorized the humans who lived in the area and, though the Little People disapproved of what Gorrodin was doing, they did nothing—for magical creatures do not fight each other.'

'Why not?' asked Duncan sourly. 'We humans dinnae have a problem killing our own.'

'I only know that this is a rule the Little People dare not break. They *must* not fight each other.' She shrugged cynically. 'And even if that rule did not exist, Galhadrians care only for music, dancing, and merriment—they do not much care about men.

'But Gorrodin had a daughter who could not bear to see the evil done by one of her own kin. When a Scots army gathered to fight the Gorrodin-Rath, she led them to a hidden cache of fairy silver, knowing full well that fairy silver was deadly to the dark creatures. The Scots forged it into weapons and armour—including one magnificent sword, Excalibur, which was given to the Scots leader Arturius.'

'Excalibur? Arturius?' Duncan interrupted. 'You mean King Arthur? I thought King Arthur was just a legend.'

'It's legends that we are speaking of,' Heather said. 'You must decide whether this one is true.' Duncan nodded solemnly and the girl continued.

'Some of the Scots led a night raid on the Gorrodin-Rath's stronghold and stole the magic artefacts. When the Gorrodin-Rath, led by their mighty war-chief Mordred, gave chase they were met by Arturius and the rest of his warriors. Gorrodin's army could not harm those Scots who wore silver armour and could themselves be killed by warriors wielding weapons made from fairy silver. Even so there was not nearly enough silver to go round and the Scots were greatly outnumbered—so the battle raged all through the night until only a handful of fighters were alive on either side. As dawn broke, the Gorrodin-Rath fled into a tunnel leading to the cavern under Arthur's Seat. Arturius, though mortally wounded, led his few remaining men into the mountain after the creatures. They sealed the entrance to the cavern with rocks and placed their silver weapons and armour in front, as a barrier to stop the Gorrodin-Rath ever getting out—even Excalibur was left there.

'The Scots melted down a few pieces of fairy silver and set them in a stout door further up the tunnel and, as a final precaution, they erected a fort at the tunnel entrance to always be ready if the

Gorrodin-Rath got out. The fort eventually became Edinburgh Castle and the hill under which Gorrodin's army were trapped was named Arthur's Seat.' Heather indicated the slope in the distance. 'Gorrodin vanished to the remote north and left his minions to their terrible fate.'

'What happened to the magic artefacts?' the highlander said. 'What happened to the girl?'

'Nobody remembers,' Heather said simply.

'That's quite a story.' Duncan felt a sinking feeling in the pit of his stomach.

'There's more,' Heather continued. 'And you won't like it.'

'No. I get the feeling I winnae,' the highlander agreed.

'The Scots also sealed up a nearby well, the only other entrance to the tunnel. Over hundreds of years, the treasure, the tunnel, Arthur, and the well drifted into legend—and the city of Edinburgh was built on top of them.'

Heather bit her lip.

'If the legend is true then it's not treasure that you're stealing. It's the bars of an ancient prison.' She held out a hand. 'Duncan, I'm sorry . . . '

But Duncan was already on his feet and running towards the Underground City.

The Battle

Peazle stood up and stamped his feet. It was definitely getting colder—too cold to sit around any longer; at least, that's what he tried to tell himself. In fact, he felt incredibly vulnerable sitting in the flickering pool of firebrand light all on his own—he hoped Shadowjack was almost finished smelting the helmet on the upper level. The pickpocket took a deep breath and this time he didn't cough. If he was careful and took things gently he could probably get that last shield back to the bottom of the well on his own. A few steps then a rest, then a few steps; the hardest part would be getting it from the top of the rock pile. He'd just wait a couple more minutes to get his breath back properly and then he'd give it a go . . .

Duncan raced through the Underground City, moving over the dark and uneven floor with the grace of a natural hunter. He powered into Shadowjack's vault and cleared the fiery forge with one leap, his foot catching the astonished blacksmith in the centre of the chest. The blow, with the force of a hundred yard run behind it, caught the giant totally by surprise and he toppled backwards with a grunt. As he crashed to the floor, Shadowjack instinctively lifted the heavy tongs to strike the boy but Duncan's knife suddenly glinted in the firelight, right below the smith's left eye.

'You make one move,' Duncan spat, his face inches from the blacksmith's own, 'and you'll never see the money you so badly wish tae spend.'

'What is this treachery, boy?' Shadowjack let go of the tongs and held up his empty hand. 'Tell me quick. I've always played fair with you.'

'You didnae tell us about the monsters!' Duncan wrapped his fingers in the blacksmith's bristling beard and pulled him even closer. 'That's why the gypsies you overheard never came looking for the treasure, isn't it? You told us about the silver, you treacherous dog, but you didnae tell us about the monsters!'

'Monsters!' the giant roared. 'What are you talking about, boy?'

'The silver guards a great evil! It cannae be taken out!'

'What?' The blacksmith's eyes were almost bulging out of his head. 'That stupid fairy story! Only an ignorant peasant would believe something like that. I didn't even think it worth mentioning!'

'Well, I believe in fairy stories,' Duncan hissed. He lifted himself off Shadowjack's chest and stood up, still brandishing the knife. 'I lost my brother to the Little People. I'm not going tae lose my best friend.'

'You're brave to anger a man like me, highlander.' Shadowjack sat up, his face red with rage. 'And also

96

very foolish.' He struggled to his feet and stepped forward, towering above Duncan.

The boy was not cowed. 'If I'm wrong then I apologize to you, blacksmith, and my shame will be great.' Duncan tucked his knife back into a little leather sheath under his arm. 'But I fear the worst.'

'Ach, nonsense!' Shadowjack fumed. 'I'm on my way down to help Peazle take out the last piece of treasure right now—when we've brought it up, I want to hear no more of this ignorant babble.'

'The last piece? Already?'

'Aye.' Shadowjack scowled. 'We're not all sitting around thinking up daft children's tales, you know. That boy down there is working like a dog.'

'Shadowjack, I beg you to trust me on this.' Duncan moved to the well. 'Stoke up the fire as high as it will go. Please.' The highlander sat himself on the edge and grasped the rope. 'I'll explain when I return. If I'm wrong, you can laugh at me while you count your money.' A self-mocking smile played on his lips but his eyes burned into Shadowjack's with an intensity that made the blacksmith suddenly look down. Then Duncan slid over the well rim and into the darkness.

Shadowjack stood for a few minutes staring at the black hole and stroking his beard. Then he turned and began to quickly pile wood on the forge.

The shield made a grinding noise as Peazle slid it down the rock pile, but he knew the silver would be undamaged by the jagged stone. He had once overheard a learned gent claim that precious metals scratched and broke easily but this stuff seemed indestructible—Peazle was beginning to doubt these learned gents were ever right about anything. The shield slid off the last rock and hit the floor with a clang and the pickpocket began to drag it down the passage that led to the bottom of the well.

He had gone about fifty yards when it occurred to him that he had left Shadowjack's liquor flask back at the rock pile and, sighing, he trudged back to get it. He was stuffing the container back inside his shirt when he heard footsteps pounding up the corridor in his direction.

'No need to hurry, Shadowjack, I'm managing just fine.' He looked round as a running figure emerged from the darkness. 'Duncan! What are you doing down here?'

Duncan slowed to a halt, his chest heaving.

'You all right?'

'Aye. Why wouldn't I be? I been coughing that's all . . .'

Peazle's reply was drowned out by a deafening crack. A slab of stone the size of the pickpocket shot out of the rock pile like a cork out of a champagne bottle, shattering into a thousand pieces on the cavern wall opposite. Duncan launched himself at Peazle, knocking him over and flattening him to the ground—the pickpocket's firebrand spun into the air and clattered across the floor as pieces of boulder rained down around them. A chunk the size of a brick hit Duncan between the shoulders and a thousand points of pain burst across the back of his head. He slumped forward on top of the pickpocket.

'Duncan! You're squashing me!' Peazle tried to roll the half-conscious highlander off—then froze as he peered out from under his friend's motionless body.

An arm jutted out of a hole where the rock had been—long and powerful and twice the size of one of Shadowjack's powerful limbs. But this arm was so white it was almost translucent—hairless, with thick blue veins and spattered with patches of grey mould. And the hand on the end! It was more like a claw— curved, twitching, and bristling with vicious yellow talons.

'Heaven save us!' Peazle whispered, thumping his groggy friend on the shoulder. 'Duncan! Get up! Pleeeeeeeeeeeeeeease!'

With a shudder the rocks around the arm rose and parted and a head and shoulders burst out. Peazle screamed. The huge cranium was bald and misshapen with eyes sunk so far into the creature's doughy flesh that they were no more than malevolent little beads. The monster pulled its body slowly out of the gap, squat, wide, and bent almost double, as if an eternity of squeezing through low passages had permanently curved the massive knotted spine. It opened a cavernous mouth, revealing two rows of gleaming jagged teeth, and stepped down from the rock pile— almost daintily—though its powerful sinewy legs ended in hooves rather than feet. Another head, equally ugly, burst from the rocks a few feet away.

'Duncan, we have to get out of here!' Peazle hissed, twisting his friend's head in the direction of the aberrations and slapping his face. 'Please, please, please!'

Duncan finally got his eyes to focus and his head jerked backwards. With a grunt of agony he pushed himself groggily to his feet, pulling Peazle up with him. By now a third, smaller creature, was forcing its way up through the stones and the first two were clear of the rock pile and standing on the chamber floor itself.

'What in God's name are they?' Peazle whimpered.

'Demons? Trolls? I dinnae ken.' The imminent danger had sharpened Duncan's senses, despite the pain. 'Whatever they are we can't let them get between us and the way back.'

The monsters were crouching and then stretching, sniffing the air and each other. Grabbing Peazle's hand the highlander began to inch along the wall. 'At least they dinnae seem to see very well.'

The two closest trolls glanced at the boys then over at the exit. With ugly leering grins they moved to block off the boys' retreat.

'Nothing wrong with their hearing, Duncan.' Peazle tried to shrink back further into the shadows, but it was too late. The third troll had now joined his companions on the floor and a fourth was beginning to emerge from the rocks.

'It's nae use. We're trapped.' Duncan pulled out his knife and held it valiantly in front of them. 'When I attack, you run to the right. Follow the wall. You'll only have a few seconds.'

'When you *attack*!' Peazle grabbed his friend's arm. 'What are you talking about?'

'Nae point in both of us dying,' Duncan said calmly despite his racing heart. 'Go to the right like I say.' The trolls looked at each other and one snorted loudly—the boys could smell the blast of fetid breath—the nearest couldn't be more than twelve feet away.

'What if they understand Scots?' Peazle stammered. 'You've just told them which way I'm going to go.'

'Then pick your own way! Surprise me!'

'No, Duncan.' The pickpocket picked up a chunk of broken stone. 'You're my only friend and, by my soul, we'll live or die together.'

The trolls edged towards the boys, hooves clicking on the stone floor and thin black lips curling back over their massive drooling teeth. They hunched down and stretched their claws out in front, grunting and panting and waving their heads from side to side. Duncan shifted the knife from hand to hand. 'Goodbye, Peazle,' he said gently.

With a mighty roar, Shadowjack Henry barrelled into the cavern swinging the silver shield around his head. The corner of the shield caught the troll nearest to him and half its malformed head vanished in a black oily cloud. The other creatures spun round, releasing a cacophony of ear-splitting screams, recoiling when they caught sight of the gleaming silver.

'To me, boys!' Shadowjack raced across the vault. The shield connected with the outstretched claw of one of the trolls and sliced it clean off—the white clutching hand flew through the air and landed at Peazle's feet. Galvanized, he and Duncan leapt out of the shadows and darted over to where Shadowjack was swinging the shield maniacally back and forth. At each thrust the monsters shrank away, waving their arms ineffectually.

'Duncan, my lad,' the blacksmith roared as the boys sheltered behind him. 'I've decided there's no need for you to apologize after all.'

'Glad tae hear it,' Duncan said as the trio began backing into the tunnel that led to the well. 'Now give me the shield.'

'What?'

'Shadowjack, you said you'd trust me! Give me the shield and I need you to do exactly what I say.' Duncan grabbed the shield before the blacksmith could object. 'Run back to the well. Take Peazle—though you might have tae carry him.' Peazle was stumbling alongside them coughing violently again. 'I've nae time to explain but I have a plan. Just climb back up to the vault and start melting the silver horseshoes in thon forge.'

'Why? I mean . . . how many?'

'All of them, Shadowjack, or else we're all dead. Go!'

The blacksmith looked as if he was about to object but an unearthly scream of rage rose from the chamber they had just left. Instead, he scooped Peazle under one meaty arm and set off towards the bottom of the well. Duncan turned and faced the direction of the enemy, shield in hand, as the pursuing trolls clattered into the tunnel. They stopped when they saw his defence and hissed and spat and screamed but dared not go any further. Duncan was facing his worst nightmare and he felt like collapsing with pain and terror, but he was a boy with a long line of warrior's blood in his veins.

'Right, ye wee Sassenach devils!' he yelled, for want of anything more appropriate to say. 'Let's see you take on a highlander! Yes, you wi' your pasty faces and bad breath!'

The trolls retreated a few feet, snarling and gurgling amongst themselves. Their bent and bloated bodies almost filled the corridor but Duncan could see at least five of them now, crowding behind the leader. Two of the monsters at the back suddenly turned and loped away, the tapping of their hooves fading into the distance. The highlander knew immediately what they were up to. There were many branching tunnels in this labyrinth—his adversaries were going to circle round and find another route to the well, catching Peazle and Shadowjack unawares and cutting off his own retreat.

There was nothing else for it. With a bloodcurdling highland yell Duncan charged at the enemy—the three remaining trolls were taken completely by surprise. Turning in panic they tried to scramble over each other, spitting and clawing in an attempt to get away, but their bodies were too large in such a confined space to manoeuvre properly. Duncan swung the shield and caught the nearest creature square in the back—a huge gout of black liquid arched from between its shoulders as it fell writhing and screaming. His second swing took the upraised arm from the second before the monsters thundered, squealing in terror, back the way they had come. Duncan shouldered the shield, spun on his heel, and headed in the direction Shadowjack had gone.

Peazle was standing shivering, knee deep in water, at the bottom of the well shaft, when Duncan reached the chamber.

'Shadowjack's at the top melting the horseshoes back down again,' he coughed weakly. 'Seems a shame after all the effort we put into making them in the first place.'

'Then get up there after him! These beasties will be here any second and I cannae hold them all off— not even with a silver shield.'

The pickpocket shook his head.

'I haven't got the strength to climb, Duncan. Besides, I thought you might need this.' He thrust his arm into the black water and pulled out a beautiful silver sword.

'Where in the name of the wee man did you get that?' Duncan gasped.

'I hid it behind a rock a couple of weeks ago, when I first found this place.' He held out the weapon. 'Out of pure greed, y'know?'

Duncan took the sword reverently.

'Peazle, you never cease tae amaze me.'

The bucket and rope came tumbling down the funnel and splashed into the water, narrowly missing the pickpocket.

'The horseshoes are melting away just fine,' Shadowjack's voice echoed down. 'Grab hold of the rope, lad.'

'Take the shield with you.' Duncan thrust it out. 'Melt it down too. Melt everything that's silver. Then throw the rope back for me.'

Too weak to protest, Peazle hoisted the shield on his back and sat on the bucket.

'Haul away, Shadowjack!' Duncan shouted.

The boy, bucket, and shield rose unhesitatingly into the air and disappeared into the chamber roof—Duncan could hear Shadowjack grunting as he pulled. The highlander turned, sword in hand, in time to see the first troll slither into the chamber. Then another entered, and another, and another, until twelve of the monstrosities were bunched together in the vault. One gestured violently and the creatures began to fan out, gurgling and slobbering, and inching in both directions along the chamber wall until, eventually, they ringed the highlander.

The boy circled on the spot, holding out the sword, but he knew he was lost. He could kill five, six, perhaps even more, but—in the end—they would overcome him by sheer weight of numbers.

The bucket landed in the water again and the trolls recoiled in surprise. That was the split second Duncan needed. He rammed his foot into it and grasped the rope with one hand.

'Pull, Shadowjack! Pull, or my life is over!'

Shadowjack gave a tremendous roar of exertion from above and Duncan shot into the air. Seeing their victim about to escape, the trolls rushed forwards en masse—the largest leaping into the air towards him, talons outstretched. Duncan swung the sword in a vicious arc and the creature's clawing arm was sliced from its body. The monster fell back into the water with a scream.

'You beasties are not gonnae have any arms left by the time we finish with you!' the highlander shouted, triumphantly, as he vanished up the funnel.

Peazle was waiting at the top to help Duncan clamber out of the well and into Shadowjack's vault. The blacksmith had simply dumped the huge smelting dish onto the red hot coals of his forge then thrown in all the horseshoes—and the highlander could see the shield dissolving into a mass of bubbling molten metal that almost reached the top of the huge container. Shadowjack gave a whistle when he saw the sword.

'That's a piece and a half, and no mistake. Can't believe we missed it the first time,' he said suspiciously, eyeing the weapon. 'You want it melted down as well?'

'I dinnae think we'd better,' said Duncan holding

up the sword in awe. 'I'm thinking this might be the legendary Excalibur itself.'

'Aye. Right.'

'I'll wager on it!'

'Could we get back to your plan, Duncan, whatever it is?' Peazle pointed down the well. 'These things are climbing.'

'Tip out the molten silver.' The highlander pointed to the dish. 'Tip it doon the well.'

'What!?' Shadowjack held up his hands in horror. 'That's our fortune!'

'And how will you spend it from your grave?'

Shadowjack groaned in disbelief then spun and grabbed a stout cudgel leaning against the wall of the vault. He rammed it into the glowing coals below the dish.

'Help me then, lads, quick now before this goes up in flames!' he shouted putting all his considerable weight on the staff. The boys ran to his side and all three pushed down as hard as they could. The container creaked slowly and lifted a few inches above the forge.

'Once more, boys, with all your might, push!'

The trio wrenched down on the staff again, grunting in pain and effort and the desperation of people whose lives hung on a thread. The huge dish rose slowly out of the forge and toppled onto its side—and half a ton of molten silver surged out of the container and flowed into the well. There was an unholy scream from inside the funnel as the liquid metal engulfed the climbing trolls and swept them back into the depths. The creatures that filled the chamber below tried to escape as the molten silver hit the river at the bottom, but it was too late. A giant cloud of steam, saturated with droplets of silver, filled the vault instantly and shot along the tunnels at the bottom, enveloping the fleeing trolls.

In a matter of seconds the Gorrodin-Rath, who had survived for a millennium and a half, were blasted out of existence.

Shadowjack, Peazle, and Duncan lay on their backs in the vault, coughing and gasping and laughing with joy.

'We did it!' Shadowjack thumped Duncan on the chest. 'Poor as church mice again, aye, but alive all the same.'

'Not exactly.' Duncan held Excalibur above his head. 'This thing has a jewel set in it the size of a hen's egg.'

'Poor or not poor, let's get out of here.' Shadowjack sat up. 'I, for one, don't intend to spend one more day locked away from daylight. Not as long as I live.' He stretched out his arm, helped Peazle to his feet then reached back for Duncan. As he did so a mournful howl rose from the depths of the well—a sound more powerful, more nerve jangling and, strangely enough, more human than any of the other trolls had made. Shadowjack froze in mid-pull.

'Oh, my God.' Peazle clutched the blacksmith's arm. 'What was that?'

'Mordred—that would be my guess,' said Duncan flatly. 'Their war chief. Clever wee beastie. He must have stayed well back while the rest attacked.'

'How do you *know* all this stuff?'

'Never mind that. What will we do?'

'Whatever it is we better do it quick!'

Shadowjack hauled Duncan onto his feet with a mighty tug. The trio could hear hoofbeats growing louder, rattling down the tunnel towards the bottom of the well. Mordred was coming.

'The dish!' The pickpocket pointed to the container lying on its side. 'There's enough silver left crusted on the bottom of the dish, inside and out, to stop what's down there ever getting past it. It looks like it might fit in the well.'

'Only one way to find out.' Shadowjack flexed his mighty arms, picked up the container with a muscle-popping heave and slammed it into the hole in the vault floor. It slid in almost to its brim but the lip prevented it sinking any further. Shadowjack stepped back waving his arms in the air.

'Ooooh. Still a bit hot, that,' he said through gritted teeth.

There was another venomous roar from the bottom of the well, then the rat-tat-tat of Mordred's hooves thundering back down the passage as the monster searched in vain for another way out of the lower level. Duncan pushed at the smelting container with his foot but it didn't budge.

'You think there's any way that . . . thing can get out?'

'I doubt it,' Peazle said. 'I been down there, remember?'

'What if someone removes this dish?'

'This vault already has a bad enough reputation. After all that unearthly screaming and drumming I can't see anyone ever coming near it again.'

'Just in case, we can block up the stairs that lead down here,' Shadowjack said.

'Wait a minute.' Peazle went to the back of the vault and fetched his journal. 'Whatever that thing trapped down there might be, it's lived for a long,

long time and it isn't likely to die anytime soon.' He opened the book and began to write. 'Gather as many loose rocks as you can to hide the well—I'm going to finish my diary and leave it here as a warning in case anyone ever finds this place again.'

'I think we should hide the sword for the same reason.' Duncan looked admiringly at the weapon. 'We just prise the jewel out of the hilt first—it's big enough to make us all wealthy.'

Shadowjack and Duncan silently scoured the vault and adjoining corridors for suitable debris while Peazle completed his journal. They wrapped the book in one of Shadowjack's smelting gloves, left it in the dish, pulled a plank over the top and covered it with the rocks.

'I told you some day you'd write something important.' Duncan patted Peazle on the shoulder.

The pickpocket didn't smile. 'I pity the poor soul who finds it,' he said.

Then, with Excalibur wrapped in an old oilskin cloth, Peazle, Duncan, and Shadowjack Henry walked out of the Underground City and into the sun.

The Bodysnatcher

Charlie turned the page but there was nothing else written in the book. He flicked through the rest of Peazle's diary but, from that point on, the journal was blank. He stood up, ignoring Lily, and paced around the theatre floor. The girl sat and waited, running a small silver ball over her fingers from one hand to another. Finally Charlie turned to her, tight lipped.

'There's no way I'm believing that,' he burst out. 'There's no way I'm believing there's some kind of monster trapped at the bottom of the Underground City.'

Lily stayed quiet.

'I know what you're thinking—that tapping I heard when I was underground was the sound of Mordred's hooves. You think he heard me and he came running up the passage below.'

'You don't know what I think.'

'Well, it's rubbish. That noise I heard was council workers digging, just like you said.'

'Could be.' Lily shrugged. 'I wasn't down there.'

'I don't believe in that kind of stuff! The journal must be a hoax.'

'Sit down, Charlie,' Lily said. 'Trying to make sense of this and walk at the same time is freaking you out.'

The boy slouched back down and patted his knees, nervously blowing out his cheeks.

'All right,' he said, after a while. 'Just suppose the diary is right. I'm just saying *suppose*, I'm not saying it *is*.' He began to get up again but Lily pulled him back down.

'All right, *suppose*,' she said. 'What are you going to do?'

'All I have to do is make sure nobody ever finds Shadowjack's vault again. I mean, Mordred's still trapped, isn't he? I'll go down and cover the smelting forge and . . . er . . . I'll hide the stairway I found that leads to the vault, put the stones back. Put everything back the way it was.' He smiled hopefully at Lily. 'If there *is* some sort of horrible creature down there, well, that'll keep him hidden for another two hundred years.'

'I suppose it would,' said Lily. 'If it wasn't for the fact that there are council workers digging straight towards him. If they break through into the bottom level Mordred will surely kill them.'

'That guy stays angry a long time, eh?'

'Worse still. He'll be out.'

'Couldn't we tell the police or the army or something?' the boy suggested.

'Tell them what? That you discovered a thousand-year-old troll living under the streets of Edinburgh? They're not likely to believe that.'

'I know the feeling.'

'You have to do something.'

'So what if he *does* get out?' Charlie was clutching

111

at straws now. 'How dangerous can he be? Magic or not, he's only one creature.'

The girl looked deep into his eyes. 'What if he breaks out when your parents are performing in the big top?'

Charlie leaped to his feet. 'What do you expect me to do? Take him on at hand-to-hand combat? I'm only a kid.'

Lily pointed to Peazle's diary. 'Two boys about your age once managed to beat a whole army of trolls.'

'With the help of a magic sword and a blacksmith the size of Mount Everest!'

With a flick of her wrist Lily sent the silver ball whizzing towards Charlie's head. He plucked it out of the air an inch from his nose, blinking in surprise.

'What the hell did you do that for?'

'Your parents are acrobats, you said? Look at how easily you caught the ball. You've inherited their speed and their eye.'

'I'd rather my parents were big game hunters and I'd inherited their guns. What am I supposed to fight this thing with, my teeth?' He gave the girl a sarcastic look. 'I've got silver fillings, think that'll help?'

Lily didn't get the joke. 'Only fairy silver will work against these kinds of creatures but you're on the right track. You have to think of what you have on your side, Charlie—not what you don't.'

'I've got you. You want to come into the Underground City with me?'

'Not a chance.'

'Thought not,' the boy said drily. 'But thanks for your support.' He flicked the ball back.

'Charlie, I didn't mean it like that!'

'I got to think about this.' Charlie strode towards the theatre exit. 'I have to go somewhere and work this out. It's not that I'm stupid or a coward.' He opened the door, letting in a flood of sunlight. 'It's just that I'm scared to death and I don't have a clue what to do.'

He stepped into the light without bothering to say goodbye. The door closed with a click, leaving Lily sitting alone in the gloomy big top. She took out some more silver balls and began to juggle them—thirteen, then fifteen, then seventeen, spinning faster and faster despite the half-light. One of the silver balls hit the edge of her finger and shot away at an awkward angle. She tried to recapture her momentum clutching at empty air, but another ball deflected off her wrist and vanished under a chair. Next moment all the balls were bouncing across the floor away from the astonished girl. Lily looked at her hands.

'Not fair,' she said to nobody in particular. 'Not fair at all.'

Charlie sat in his room at the boarding house—he had been there for hours staring at the wall, though his parents had interrupted him a couple of times and tried unsuccessfully to make conversation.

'It's Wednesday tomorrow,' his father had said. 'Big top's shut so we thought about taking you on a day trip. There's a pencil museum in Lerwick.'

'I'd love to go,' Charlie said.

'Really? You would?'

'Yes, but I can't.' Charlie thought fast. 'I . . . er . . . have to meet a girl.'

'A girl, eh?' said his father. 'You think a girl will be more fun than a pencil museum?'

'Don't tease the boy.' Charlie's mum somersaulted onto the bed beside her son and they both bounced up and down for a few seconds. 'What would you like to know about the facts of life?'

'Nothing, mother. We'll probably just go for a Coke.'

'Ah, young love.' His mum nudged him, wrinkling her nose. 'Do you think about her a lot?'

'As a matter of fact I've thought about nothing else all evening.' Charlie looked up at his mother. 'And I don't think she's been very honest. I think she's been using me.'

'Aw, baby.' His mum suddenly looked serious, which didn't happen very often. 'Are you going to be all right? You want to talk about it?'

For a second Charlie considered telling his parents the whole story—just giving them Peazle's journal to read and then climbing into bed and going to sleep—letting *them* work out what was real and what was not and what he should do. He looked at his father hopefully. His father made a high whinnying noise, his cheeks vibrating violently.

'That's my impression of a horse,' he said. 'I can only do it out of one side of my mouth.'

Charlie turned to his mother.

'It's fine,' he said, patting her hand. 'Everything's OK.'

'You have a talk with this young lady—don't let her walk all over you.'

'I don't intend to.'

'Good. Well, you have a fun time tomorrow. Dad and I can have a long lie and go shopping instead.'

Charlie's dad sighed.

Finally his parents went to bed and left Charlie to his thoughts. He was sick to his stomach about what he had learned and had racked his brains in vain for a logical explanation. He felt betrayed by Lily, even though he hardly knew her. And he felt lonely. He had come to think of Peazle and Duncan as friends and now that the diary was finished he would never know what happened to them. Did they take the jewel from Excalibur to Glasgow and sell it? Did they become rich like they had dreamed? Or had Peazle succumbed to the illness that was obviously killing him?

Charlie opened the pickpocket's diary and flicked through it again. At the back was the hand-drawn map of Greyfriars graveyard—there were little ticks scattered across the page, presumably marking the sites of recently buried corpses ripe for stealing. Looking closer at the map he suddenly noticed that one plot was marked with a tiny cross rather than a tick. He held the book closer and peered at the minuscule marking. Was it a cross?

Or was it a sword?

Then suddenly Charlie knew exactly where Excalibur was.

He leaped to his feet, opened the boarding house window, climbed onto the sill and, without a second's hesitation, swung out and clambered down the drainpipe. Soon he was walking through the silent, deserted streets once more—his mind in turmoil. He reached the big top, let himself in and felt his way to the little vault in the South Bridge where the workmen kept their tools. He took one of the construction helmets with a light on top, put it on his head and wrapped a short shovel in a splattered paint sheet. Then he let himself out of the theatre again and strode through the Old Town until he stood at the gates of Greyfriars graveyard.

The cemetery looked very different at night—the church seemed to be carved from squat cold shadows and gravestones were scattered across the inky lawns like blackened stumps of teeth. Charlie switched on the torch and made his way quietly round the church until he came to the grave of Allan Ramsay, hidden in thick shadow at the bottom of the building. Hands shaking, he unwrapped the shovel, looking around to see if his actions might be detected. But the graveyard was deserted and all the lights were off in the surrounding tenements. He opened Peazle's journal at the back and studied the exact position of the cross.

'Here we go,' the boy muttered, 'the last of the bodysnatchers.'

He took a deep breath, plunged the shovel into the soil a few feet from the flat tombstone, and began to dig.

He worked in silence, trying to keep his breathing as quiet as possible—he didn't want anyone sneaking up behind him while he was busy digging up a grave in the middle of the night. Soon there was a mound of earth beside him and a widening hole at his feet.

Suddenly the point of the shovel hit something solid.

'Please don't let that be someone's head,' Charlie muttered, digging tentatively round the spot—but the object he was uncovering glinted in his helmet beam. It was made of metal. The sky was beginning to lighten so he scraped hurriedly at the dirt and soon he had uncovered a beautiful sword handle.

Hardly daring to breathe he bent down, grasped the handle and pulled. Excalibur slid slowly and easily from the soil next to the grave of Peazle's hero and Charlie held the dirt-covered weapon aloft, saluting his companions from the past.

'You did hide the sword!' he laughed, wiping dirt from the hilt with his sleeve. 'You took the jewel and left the sword in case someone else needed to . . . use it.' His voice trailed away as the last of the graveyard earth fell from the hilt.

The jewel was still there, gleaming in its silver setting.

He sat down on Allan Ramsay's tombstone, looking at the beautiful sword and a great feeling of sadness welled up inside him. Partly he was uncertain and scared. Partly he couldn't understand how he had got into an incredible situation like this. But mostly he was sad for Peazle. He didn't know why the jewel was buried with the sword—but the fact that it was still there meant that Peazle, Shadowjack, and Duncan couldn't have got rich after all—and without money the pickpocket wouldn't have been able to afford proper medicine. Charlie didn't think Peazle would have lasted much longer after finishing his diary.

The boy felt a welcome warmth at his back as the sun began to rise over the eastern wall of the graveyard. He raised Excalibur above his head and let the rays of a new day dance along its blade.

'Thank you, my friend,' he whispered.

He stood up and made a few practice cuts in the

air with the weapon. He had no idea how to wield a sword but Excalibur was light and somehow it felt right in his hand. He edged his way round Ramsay's grave, slashing at imaginary foes, imagining he was Arturius, surrounded by the army of the Gorrodin-Rath. He clutched his heart.

'You got me, you pesky varmints!' he croaked staggering backwards and forwards. 'But before I die I'll chase you down to the very gates of hell and seal you in.'

Charlie stopped, Excalibur quivering in the air.

'I don't get it.' He lowered the sword and frowned. 'Why would the Gorrodin-Rath retreat into a tunnel where they knew they could be trapped? Why didn't they just run away?'

He thought back to Peazle's diary.

As dawn broke, the Gorrodin-Rath finally fled and took shelter in the caverns under Arthur's Seat.

Charlie looked at the golden orb getting higher over the graveyard wall.

As dawn broke.

Of course. A grin of comprehension spread slowly across his face.

There was something else the Gorrodin-Rath feared as much as fairy silver.

They were afraid of daylight.

The Monster

Charlie stepped into the theatre, construction helmet in one hand and paint cloth in the other. Lily was sitting in the empty front row of chairs exactly where the boy had left her the evening before, her face pale and drawn. She looked as if she had been there all night.

'Where's your father, Lily?' Charlie said.

'What?' The girl was taken aback by the unexpected question. '*I* don't know.'

'I mean, where's your father on *that*?' The boy pointed to a huge poster adorning the theatre wall. It advertised the acts performing at the big top during the festival and was printed in fancy, circus-style lettering.

'I remember my dad telling me this theatre is just for acrobats—apart from Deekie-Bob the Wonder Dog, of course.' He walked over and studied the poster more closely. 'You said your father was a magician performing in this big top. I don't see your father advertised here.'

119

'My father *is* a magician,' Lily protested.

'How did you know that ordinary silver wouldn't work against Mordred?' Charlie kept going.

'What are you talking about?'

'Yesterday, you said that *only* fairy silver could beat Mordred. How did you know that?'

Lily threw up her hands. 'I didn't! It was a guess.'

'It didn't sound like a guess.' Charlie strode towards her. 'Why do I never see you anywhere except inside this theatre? How come you know so much about Edinburgh's past?'

'Why are you hounding me like this?' Lily backed away from him.

'You said your father is a great magician. Where is he?'

120

'Stop!' The girl held up her hands but the boy kept advancing.

'You're Gorrodin's daughter, aren't you?' He pointed an accusing finger. 'You're one of the Little People. You're the girl who led the Scots to the fairy silver and you've been hanging around ever since. And you're Heather, the girl Duncan liked—I'm right, aren't I?'

'You seem to have it all worked out.' Lily managed to sound impressed and resentful at the same time.

'Actually it was a guess.' Charlie looked sheepish.

'It was a good guess.'

The boy just shrugged. It seemed as if nothing was impossible any more. He would just have to get used to it.

'The diary said Heather had dark hair but yours is red. I suppose that was magic?'

'No. It was dirt. You think nineteenth-century gypsies could afford shampoo?'

Charlie laughed despite himself. He reached out and took her arm. She flinched as if she wasn't used to being touched.

'It's all right. Sit beside me.' Despite her deceit the boy found it impossible to stay angry with Lily and, besides, he needed answers fast—any information he could get from the girl might now save his life. He flopped down on a chair and she sat next to him, looking at the floor.

'Why have you stayed here so long?' Charlie said. 'Why don't you live in Galhadria with the rest of the Little People?'

'I don't know.'

'No? You've had over a thousand years to come up with a reason.'

'I don't . . . remember.' The girl looked genuinely unsure. 'It was so long ago.' Lily still didn't look up. 'My father . . . '

'Where exactly *is* he?'

'I . . . I don't know that either.' She was almost whispering now. 'He brought me from Galhadria to this world and then he deserted me.'

'I'm sorry about that.' Charlie took her hand.

'I loved my father. Perhaps I wanted to make better what he did wrong.'

The boy squinted at her. 'Are you telling me you've hung around the entrance to the Underground City for a millennium just to stop Mordred and his gang getting out?'

The girl put a trembling hand to her mouth. 'I thought . . . some day my father might come back for me,' she said finally.

'I got to admire your patience.' Charlie gave her hand a squeeze. Then he let it go. 'Lily,' he said, as evenly as he could, 'why won't you use your powers to kill Mordred? Why are you trying to make me do it instead?'

Lily finally looked up, her eyes wide and green. 'Magical creatures *must* not fight other magical creatures—it's a law so old that we no longer even think about it.' She leaned forward earnestly. 'But we know that if we break it something *terrible* will happen. We just *know*.' She shook her head and her red curls bobbed violently. 'I can't help you.'

'I know, I know.' The boy couldn't hide his irritation. 'And Little People don't interfere with humans either. For a magical race you Galhadrians don't actually *do* an awful lot.'

'You're not even supposed to know we *exist*.' Lily

squeezed her mortal companion's hand so tightly the boy winced. 'Charlie, I'm doing my best! I've kept people out of Mordred's way for centuries. Now I'm trying to save the lives of these workmen.'

'Yeah. By sending me instead.'

Lily sighed deeply. 'Mordred is proof that magic exists. If he gets out your race will once again believe. But things are not like they used to be on earth. Men might actually have the power to make magic work for *them*.'

Charlie frowned. 'And that would be so bad?'

'You've developed weapons that could destroy your own world, Charlie—and that's without magic,' Lily said sadly. 'What do you think?'

The boy picked up the paint cloth and unwrapped Excalibur—the blade glowed a ghostly blue in the dim light of the big top. Lily gasped when she saw it.

'There's no point hanging around here then, is there?' he said, lifting the sword above his head and plunging it back down. The blade sank into the stone floor as if it were made of butter—Charlie let go and Excalibur quivered and sang, vibrating like a huge bee-sting. 'I've got a monster to fight.'

'Do you have a plan?'

'Of course.' Charlie stood up and placed the helmet with the flashlight on his head. 'I'm counting on Mordred laughing himself to death when he sees me.'

'Let me fix this.' Lily rose and fastened the strap of the hard-hat under the boy's chin. She had to stand on her toes to reach and the top half of her body pressed against his chest. She felt cold.

'So what do I call you now?' Charlie said. 'A Little Person?'

'You call me a friend,' she said looking into his eyes. Then she slid her arms round his waist and gave him a tentative hug, her head resting lightly on his shoulder.

'You have your parents' courage,' she whispered in his ear. 'Remember you also have their skill. Use it.' She leaned back and kissed him quickly on the lips—then held him by the shoulders at arm's length, like a general inspecting one of her troops. Charlie was surprised to see the girl's eyes glistening with tears.

'If I don't manage this . . . ' he began, but Lily put a finger to his lips.

'These are the first tears I have shed since my father vanished,' she said softly—and suddenly the boy felt more confident, more powerful, and more loved than he ever had in his life. He lifted his hand to touch the girl's cheek just once—then turned and walked towards the door at the back of the theatre.

'Your sword!' Lily motioned towards Excalibur, still upright and vibrating.

'I don't need it. Not yet.' Charlie smiled and stepped through the door.

Lily came back to the sword and crouched down beside it, admiring the intricate carvings on the flawless blade. She clenched her fists in a little gesture of triumph.

'He does have a plan,' she said to Excalibur. 'I knew he would.'

Charlie searched around the little vault where the council workers kept their supplies until he found a small pulley that he had noticed on his first visit. He put it in his pocket, took a length of nylon rope from a shelf and wound it round his waist. Then he moved the debris covering the tunnel entrance, slid inside and began crawling back towards the lower levels of the Underground City. He knew he could easily find Shadowjack Henry's vault again—all he had to do was follow the chalk marks he had made on the wall less than a week ago.

Less than a week ago—he just couldn't believe it. Just seven days ago he was an ordinary boy living an ordinary life and now he was marching down a hidden tunnel to do battle with an ancient monster. He wasn't that same boy any more—the old Charlie wouldn't even have stood up to a school bully. Lily was sure that magic would be disastrous to men and, reluctantly, he was forced to agree with her. This was not some petty classroom squabble but a noble and valiant quest that might even save his whole race.

He still wasn't sure it was worth fighting a monster for.

When he reached Shadowjack's vault the boy stood outside the doorway for several minutes until his breathing was under control and his heart had stopped pounding like a jackhammer. Once he was inside the vault he would have to work quickly and calmly if he was to have any chance of succeeding— or staying alive, for that matter.

'Hesitation is an acrobat's worst enemy,' he said to himself and stepped into the chamber.

The hard-hat's beam lit up the wooden triangle and iron hook at the base of the vault wall—the old apparatus that Shadowjack Henry once used to draw water for his forge. Charlie dragged it to within a few feet of the well, positioning the apparatus between the blocked-up hole and vault doorway. He unwound the rope from around his waist, threaded it through the detachable metal pulley he took from his pocket and fastened the pulley to the wooden triangle. Then he took the end of the rope that had been threaded through the pulley and tied it to the ancient hook—the metal was old and rusty but still solid enough for his purpose. The rope and pulley system now formed the basis for a crude winch and he slid the hook under the rim of the metal cylinder that blocked the well. He stepped back, wound the rest of the rope back round his waist, then turned and began walking towards the vault exit.

The rope tightened. Charlie gritted his teeth and kept going. The pulley jiggled and there was a grinding sound from the metal dish. The boy pulled harder, though each tug tightened the rope around his waist and forced air from his lungs. The metal dish groaned again and the rim slid up a few inches. Charlie grunted, trying to find a proper foothold, throwing himself against the rope, fighting for air, sweat prickling his body. His feet slipped with each step so that he seemed to be walking on the spot, but he bent his head and strained even more. The dish rose a foot out of the well.

'Aaaaaaaaaaaaaaaaaaaargh!' Charlie roared, staggering forwards, fists clenched, veins standing out on his forehead. 'Come on! You rotten, stupid dish . . . COME ON!'

With a horrendous screech the metal container lurched out of the hole in the ground and landed with a crash, demolishing the wooden frame. Charlie collapsed face down, his outstretched hands scraping along the floor of the vault, lacerating the skin on his palms. In an instant he was back on his feet and unwinding the rope. He glanced over his shoulder— the metal dish lay on its side and right behind it the boy could see a gaping black hole in the vault floor.

The well was open.

The boy listened. At first the only thing he could hear was his own ragged breathing, but then he caught a noise, faint and far away, a noise that sounded like drumming.

Mordred was coming.

Charlie darted out of the vault and sped back through the tunnels. His arms and legs were pumping with all their might, but he concentrated on keeping his neck rigid and the beam of light steady and pointed down—if he stumbled and fell on the uneven floor he would lose precious seconds—and that might make the difference between life and death.

A blood curdling roar echoed through the corridors behind him and, with a cry of fear, Charlie sprinted even faster. Reaching the bottom of the steps he scrabbled up, slipping on the wet stone, using his hands to propel himself forwards. But he was going too fast to judge distance properly. As he launched himself through the little hole at the top his helmet cracked on the jagged brickwork and the light smashed, plunging him into utter blackness.

Charlie's bout of terrified swearing was drowned out by another monstrous bellow, much closer than the last. The boy scrambled to his feet and began stumbling along the corridor, one arm scraping along the wall, the other waving blindly in front. The best he could now manage was a hesitant shuffle and he knew that Mordred would catch him long before he reached the big top. He didn't even know *how* to get back now for he couldn't see where the tunnels forked never mind the chalked numbers telling him which passage to take.

The trembling boy stopped, taking deep breaths, trying desperately to calm down. Wiping tears from his eyes, he peered into the blackness in a vain attempt to see something, *anything*, that might give him a clue where the next turn-off lay.

And there it was—a glowing pinpoint of light punching a tiny hole in the darkness! Letting go of the wall the boy staggered towards the glow, arms flailing in front of him, his stumbling run gathering momentum until it ended in a headlong dive. His lungs emptied with a painful whoosh as he landed heavily on the rough floor but his outstretched fingers closed round a little sparkling object.

It was a juggling ball. And next to it was a hand-held torch.

'Thank *you*, Lily!' the boy breathed, switching on the light. The beam lit up a numbered fork to his left. It was only two feet away.

There was another howl from Mordred, this time right behind Charlie. Then the boy was off again, racing up the passages, hurling himself round dark corners and crawling along the last narrow tunnel like a jet-propelled mole. He burst into the maintenance vault, tearing the construction helmet from his head and flinging it across the room— already he could hear a horrific rending of stone as something much larger, and a thousand times stronger than he was, forced itself into the other end of the tunnel. Then Charlie was in the big top and running for the exit, grasping at Excalibur as he went past. The sword slid from the stone as easily as it had gone in and seconds later the boy was standing with his back to the theatre door, the weapon held defensively in front of his face.

The door that led to the workman's vault flew off its hinges in an explosion of shattered wood and Mordred stepped into the big top.

'Oh, my God.' Charlie's face turned chalk white as he saw his opponent for the first time. Mordred was the height of a reasonably tall man—but there any resemblance with humanity stopped. He had heavily muscled arms that reached almost to his knees and his spade-like hands ended in a rash of vicious yellow talons. The creature's legs were short and thick, there were hooves where his feet should have been and his body was maggot white, hairless and laced with thick blue veins.

But it was his face that shocked Charlie most. Mordred's angular head was bald and his jaw jutted forward like a mechanical scoop lined with dozens of little piranha-like teeth. His ears were disproportionately large, set flat against his smooth scalp—but the rest of his features were almost non-existent. His nose was no more than a hole in the front of his face and his eyes had retreated far into his skull—two glowing points of hatred burning deep within his waxy flesh. The creature took a few lurching steps towards the boy, raising its talons as it approached. Charlie lifted his sword over his head and pointed it towards the beast, like he had seen ninjas do in Kung-Fu movies. He hoped it looked impressive.

'You're not getting past me; I don't care how big

you are.' He tried to sound bold and manly but the words came out as a series of trembling squeaks. 'You never heard of David and Goliath?'

The monster stopped. A strange gurgling sound rose from somewhere inside its chest and the jutting mouth split into a hideous upturned slash. Charlie realized with a growing horror that the creature was *laughing*.

Then things got worse.

'Brave boy,' the troll gurgled. 'Brave. Even if you do hold the Great Sword.' Mordred's speech was thick and vibrant, buzzing like a swarm of feasting flies and, despite his horror, Charlie was surprised to notice that the creature had a Scottish accent. The boy gripped the sword handle tighter—it occurred to him that Mordred hadn't spoken to anyone in two centuries—he might be inclined to chat for a while before tearing the boy limb from limb. Mordred looked around the big top with what Charlie presumed was a satisfied grin.

'I cannot pass you while you have the weapon, as you surely know,' he hissed. 'But I do not need a door to escape. The poor walls of this dwelling are not like the thick stone of the prison where I suffered so long.' He headed for the side of the big top, ignoring the boy. 'I shall tear my way out with bare hands.'

The boy kept quiet, Excalibur tight in his trembling fist. Mordred raised a taloned claw. Charlie held his breath. The creature stopped, sniffing suspiciously at the air around the wall. He turned his white, mottled head and stared malevolently at the boy. The hair rose on the back of Charlie's neck.

'Clever. Soooo clever,' the troll growled. 'It is

daylight outside, is it not? You tried to fool Mordred, clever little boy.' He cantered back over to the centre of the theatre, clicking his talons together as if considering his situation.

'Clever little boy,' he muttered again. 'But Mordred can wait for night to fall. After all, I have waited for sixteen centuries to be free. Can you imagine that, little boy?'

Charlie shook his head.

'No. Mordred can hardly imagine it himself—nor does he want to.' The troll hunkered down in the middle of the big top. 'After such a time I can wait a few more hours, heh?' And he laughed his bitter, gurgling laugh again.

'I'll fight you,' Charlie said in a tiny voice. His legs were trembling so badly that he could hardly stand and he felt sick and dizzy with fear. 'Like you said, I have the Sword.'

'A Galhadrian is behind this,' the creature whispered, tapping its head with a claw. 'You would not do this on your own.' It clicked its talons together again and rose to its feet. 'Stalemate,' it hissed. 'I cannot defeat you, that is true, but you cannot catch me. At nightfall Mordred shall simply tear his way through these puny walls to freedom— you cannot guard every exit.' He turned and began to plod towards the back of the theatre.

'I don't intend to,' said Charlie quietly, looking up. Six feet above his head the safety net for the high-wire acts stretched from one side of the big top to the other. He bent his trembling knees, tensing all the muscles in his body, and leapt into the air, slashing as high as the sword could reach. Excalibur's blade swept though the steel ropes fastening the net to the wall as if they were thread. With a loud twang, one side of the mesh swept down, draping itself over Mordred.

Charlie charged forward with a yell as the creature spun round, snarling. Though the safety net was made of wire and coated with toughened rubber, the creature's talons sliced through the mesh as easily as Excalibur had. Mordred's arm shot through the hole torn in the fabric and grasped one of the metal posts that roped off the performance area. He plucked it from the theatre floor as if it were a weed, the securing bolts popping out of the concrete like bullets, and flung the spike at the boy. Charlie dived as the post rocketed towards him, hunching his shoulders and tucking in his head the way he had seen his parents do a hundred times before. The metal bar whizzed past, inches over his head and buried itself in the theatre wall—Charlie rolled out of the dive in time to see Mordred reaching for another post. With a grunt he threw Excalibur straight at the creature. Mordred roared in defiance and launched himself sideways, rolling as effectively as Charlie had done—though the movement tangled him even more in the safety net. Excalibur sliced harmlessly past and clattered away to the back of the theatre, stopping next to the door that led back into the tunnels.

Now Mordred was between Charlie and his only weapon.

'The boy has lost the Great Sword!' he cackled, slicing at the net again. 'The boy is lost.'

But instead of turning back Charlie headed straight for Mordred. The creature slashed wildly at the net, trying to free its arms properly and its jagged rows of teeth slavered as it bit down on the wire strands.

With every atom of his strength Charlie leaped again, arms outstretched like a soaring bird, up over Mordred's head. The monster thrust one tangled arm skyward, claws glinting, but Charlie tucked his head down again and flicked his legs over his back. With a grace and skill that would have delighted his parents he twisted in the air, arching over Mordred's outstretched arm, somersaulting perfectly and landing on his feet on the other side of the monster. Momentum kept him going and he staggered to the back of the theatre, grabbed Excalibur from the floor, jumped and slashed again—the other side of the safety net pinged away from the wall and enveloped the creature once more. With a ferocious howl Mordred tore into the new mesh folds with teeth and claws.

Charlie reached down to a prop table, half hidden in the shadows, and picked up a small black box. He pointed it at the big top roof.

'Welcome to the twenty-first century,' he said, the tremble gone from his voice—and pressed a green button.

With an electronic whirr the two halves of the theatre roof began to separate. Mordred's head shot up and he gave a wail as a line of sunlight appeared on the theatre floor. He struggled out of the net and lumbered towards the back of the theatre, but now Charlie and Excalibur stood between him and the only way back into the tunnels. Behind the creature a widening band of light danced and sparkled on the chrome and plastic of the theatre fittings.

The monster looked at Charlie, clasping its clawed hands together as if in prayer. Tiny eyes, filled now with sadness and fear, burned into the boy and

Charlie felt a sharp pain in his chest—just for a second he had seen something terribly human in that stare.

'Clever little boy,' Mordred whispered softly as the sunlight reached him.

Charlie's eyes widened in horror. Watching the light hit Mordred was like witnessing some huge deformed snowman caught in an inferno—the troll dissolved in front of his eyes, gobbets of flesh sliding from his body and hissing and bubbling like fat melting in a pan. Turning his head upwards and stretching out his mighty arms, Mordred let out one last agonized roar.

'MORGANAAAAAAAAAAAAAAAAAAAAAA!'

The sound echoed round and round the big top, but Mordred was gone, leaving nothing but a pool of rancid flesh on the theatre floor.

Charlie dropped Excalibur, his chest heaving.

'Well, Dad was right,' he said, as his whole body began to shake. 'This trip has certainly brought me out of my shell.'

He sank to his knees and began to cry.

The Thin Place

Charlie's palms hurt, though they had finally stopped bleeding. His crying had dried up too and he sat quietly in the middle of the big top floor looking like an exhausted clown—face and hair white from the dust in the Underground City and the knees and elbows of his clothes worn away by crawling through the tunnel. His dishevelled appearance fitted the surroundings perfectly. The door to the workmen's vault lay scattered in pieces across the theatre floor and so did bits of Mordred. There was a metal pole sticking out of the big top wall and the roof was gaping open to the sun.

The roof! Charlie leapt to his feet, pointed the remote control and clicked. With a grinding sound the metal flanges high above closed again—anyone outside would simply presume the mechanism was being tested. The boy looked at his watch and was surprised to see it was still only 7.30 a.m. Good. Not many people would be about, especially in this quiet little street—hopefully Mordred's dying yell would be mistaken for the Geronimo-style roar of a practising acrobat.

The boy was so exhausted he could hardly think

straight, but getting out of the wrecked theatre undetected certainly seemed a priority. He wondered where Lily was. He gave the control box for the big top roof a wipe with his T-shirt in case the police were inclined to fingerprint it, then prised Excalibur into the gap between the door frame and the theatre door and sliced through the hasp of the lock—now investigators might think the big top had been broken into and vandalized. Charlie wrapped the sword in the paint cloth and stuck his head nervously out of the door. Nobody was about. He hurried up the sunlit wynd and turned the corner onto the High Street without seeing another soul.

At this time in the morning even the High Street was quiet and the few passers-by didn't pay much attention to Charlie's tousled hair and torn clothes— the Festival was filled with performers dressed in weird and wonderful costumes to promote their shows. Right now there was a man dressed as a penguin on the other side of the street.

He had to figure out what to do with Excalibur. The sword was worth a fortune, he had no doubt about that, but what use was that to him? If he tried to sell it there would be all sorts of awkward questions—like what was a young boy doing with a two-thousand-year-old sword made of a metal that science couldn't explain? And, if Lily was right, the sword wasn't meant for human eyes any more than Mordred was.

The fairest thing the boy could think of was to put Excalibur back where he found it. The graveyard was bound to be empty at this time of day—he could go there right now, replace the sword, and be back in his bed before his parents even woke up. Tucking Excalibur under his arm he headed for Greyfriars.

When he arrived, there was a small figure standing just outside the wrought-iron gates, pressed against the wall as if trying to stay hidden from anyone in the cemetery.

'Lily?' Charlie said, surprised.

'Get over here.' Lily motioned nervously to him. When he got close enough she reached out and pulled him away from the gates. 'Are you all right?'

'Mordred's dead.' Charlie tapped his hand on the paint cloth, sharing the credit with the hidden sword.

'I guessed that—otherwise you wouldn't be standing here.' She clasped the boy's arm and shook it triumphantly. 'You are something else, you know that?'

'Thank you.' Charlie blushed, but so much white dust was caked on his face that Lily didn't notice.

'Where are you going now? Are you going to put the sword back?' she whispered.

'Yes, I am,' said the boy proudly.

'Not so loud!' Lily hissed. 'Listen. It's all very noble, what you're doing, but it's not a great idea for you to go in there.'

'Why not? I've been in before.'

'Exactly!' Lily said, glancing around nervously. 'You saw a white hawk with black-tipped wings and there's no doubt that it saw you.'

'So what?' Charlie screwed up his face. 'I'm not a dormouse.'

'The hawk is a lookout.' Lily glanced up quickly at the clear blue sky. 'For us. For the Little People! Greyfriars is a Thin Place, Charlie. You know what that is?'

'I remember from Peazle's diary, yeah.' The boy thought for a second. 'It's a place where the line between this world and Galhadria is almost non-existent.'

'My people are *determined* to remain a secret to humans,' Lily said. 'They let you take the sword in the hope you'd defeat Mordred and you've certainly done that.' She pointed at the paint cloth. 'But what do you think will happen if you go waltzing back in there now? They'll know you've killed him—you've got bits of troll stuck to your boots . . . '

Charlie looked down. 'Oh yeah. Think that'll come off?'

'Even worse, you worked out who *I* am.' The girl looked at him imploringly. 'Humans aren't supposed to know we exist, remember. You go in there and you'll never come out again.'

Charlie scowled. 'You Galhadrians aren't exactly big on gratitude, are you?'

'No, we're not.' It was Lily's turn to go red. 'As you so perceptively put it, we aren't big on anything except dancing, singing, and enjoying ourselves. Helping others isn't high on our agenda.'

'Then why don't you take the sword in for me?' The boy held out the weapon.

'I can't!' Lily stepped back, glancing round again. 'I'm sure my people don't approve of me hanging around on earth. If I set foot in there they'd make me go back to Galhadria with them.'

'What's wrong with that?' Charlie pushed the sword at her again. 'You've put right what your father did wrong. Well, you used *me* to put it right.'

'I *had* to, Charlie!'

'I understand.' He patted her arm. 'But while I'm

being blunt . . . ' He looked apologetic. 'Lily, I don't think your father is ever coming back.'

'Neither do I,' Lily said sadly. 'I hoped some day he might return to rescue his followers. Or even come back for me.' She sighed, and a sudden cold wind rustled through the gate. 'But, as you said, we Galhadrians aren't big on gratitude.'

'Well, I'm human.' Charlie tucked the sword back under his arm. 'And I'm putting Excalibur back where it belongs.' He pushed at the gate and the iron lattice swung open with a creak.

'Charlie.' Lily hesitated, and then stepped away from the wall. She fished in her pocket, brought out a small silver whistle and handed it to him. 'If you're ever in trouble, I mean *real* trouble, just blow. This time I'll be there. I promise.'

'What about your no-interfering-with-humans rule?'

'Let's just say I owe you.'

'I think I know why you want to stay on earth.' The boy grinned and gave her a knowing wink. 'After all this time, you're more human than Galhadrian.'

'And you're more magical than any human I ever met.' She threw her arms round the boy and hugged him tight—he held her awkwardly with one arm, the other still clutching the paint cloth.

'Goodbye, Charlie,' she whispered. 'I hope someday we'll meet again.'

Then she turned and ran. Halfway down the street, she gave a small skip. Charlie watched her, heading further and further into the distance, until she looked just like any other little girl in the world.

The shovel was where Charlie had left it, lying next to Allan Ramsay's grave. The boy unwrapped Excalibur and stood over the denuded area where, the night before, he had scraped away the soil. There was a large flat rock, half hidden under dirt—probably a remnant of a headstone that had fallen over and been covered—but the boy knew Excalibur's power and he plunged the sword down anyway. It sank easily through the stone and the packed earth below, right up to its hilt—Charlie hoped it hadn't gone through the remains of Allan Ramsay as well. He bent over to pick up the shovel—once he had covered the handle Excalibur would remain hidden for many years to come.

'Well, well, there's an old friend,' said a voice at his ear.

He spun round. To his amazement, two boys were standing right behind him—one short and thin, the other tall and muscular with long black hair. But it was their clothes that gave Charlie the biggest start—the short boy wore a bright yellow waistcoat, plus-fours, and a bowler hat, and the taller one was resplendent in full highland regalia.

'We wanted to give you a proper welcome,' said the bowler hat. 'So we dressed up in our finest togs.'

'Aye, we didn't want to scare you,' added the one with the kilt.

Having just won at hand-to-hand combat with a vicious monster Charlie was more astonished than alarmed. He simply stared, his mouth hanging open.

The shorter boy stepped forward.

'The name's Peazle,' he said. 'And this is my friend Duncan.' He shook Charlie's unresisting hand. 'Pleased to make your acquaintance.'

140

'I know who you are.' Charlie's face twisted into an incredulous smile. 'I recognize you. I don't know how I do. I just do.' He let go of Peazle's hand. 'I can't believe this. Are you ghosts? You feel solid enough.'

'Oh, we're real,' Duncan laughed and Peazle giggled as well.

'How can that be?' The boy was as delighted as he was mystified.

'It's quite a . . . eh . . . strange explanation,' said Peazle. 'I take it you read the diary?'

Charlie nodded.

'What did you think of the writing style? You can be honest.'

'Peazle!' The highlander glowered at his friend. 'Just tell the story.'

'Yes. Sorry. Well, when we beat the Gorrodin-Rath . . . ' Peazle hooked his thumbs into his waistcoat in preparation for his tale.

'*Most* of the Gorrodin-Rath,' Duncan broke in, nodding graciously at Charlie and the boy beamed with pride.

'Most of the Gorrodin-Rath,' Peazle continued. 'Anyway, we came here afterwards with Shadowjack to bury the sword. And we wanted a secluded place to get the jewel out of the hilt.'

'What happened?' Charlie sat down on Allan Ramsay's tomb, enthralled—he was going to hear the end of Peazle and Duncan's story at last.

'We were starting to prise the jewel loose, when we were surrounded by a group of Little People—and they're not so little, let me tell you.'

'They told us that Excalibur had not finished its work on earth.' Peazle sighed. 'Unfortunately its work required the jewel to stay in the hilt.'

141

'They didn't trust us not to come back and dig it up later,' Duncan added. 'So they took us back to Galhadria with them, Shadowjack as well.'

Peazle shrugged. 'We've been there ever since.'

'But you're still young.'

'That's the great thing about living with magical people.' Peazle smiled. 'Long life and good health. I've had two hundred years to study—more than anyone on earth. I always wanted to be a man of learning.' The pickpocket sat on the tomb next to Charlie and put his arm round the boy's shoulder. 'There's *so* much I want to discuss with you—I'm particularly interested in mapping genomes and DNA splicing.' Peazle's eyes were bright with excitement. 'How broad is your knowledge of genetic engineering? You must have seen programmes about it on your marvellous invention, the television?'

'Not unless they made it into a cartoon.'

Peazle sighed. Charlie turned to Duncan.

'What have *you* been up to for two hundred years?'

'Looking for my brother.' There was a long, uncomfortable silence. 'The Galhadrians claim to have nae knowledge of him,' the highlander said coldly. 'I search their land anyway.'

Charlie removed Peazle's arm from his shoulder and stood up. 'So what are you both doing here?' he asked warily.

'Like us, you know too much about the existence of the Little People.' Duncan stood straight and tall and his expression was impossible to read. 'We've been sent to bring you back with us to Galhadria.'

'I'd rather not actually.' The boy began to back away.

'They thought we would be the best ones to fetch you,' Peazle said sheepishly. 'It's not so bad there, really; Galhadria is beautiful and I owe the little people my life. The Galhadrians are courteous enough to us and don't interfere in our lives.' The boy was talking rapidly, trying to convince himself as much as Charlie. 'There are rivers and mountains for Duncan and books for me to read and we can look after you.'

'Not a chance.' The boy shook his head vehemently. 'I don't want to sound mean but you were both orphans living in poverty. I actually have a life.'

'Charlie, they'll take you whether you want to go or not.'

'Then they'll have a fight on their hands,' Charlie spat. 'I'm out of here.'

'ENOUGH!'

The voice was low and clear and seemed to come from thin air. There was a sudden shimmer above Ramsay's grave, like a heat haze, then the area around the tomb seemed to rupture—a narrow shaft of white light split the fabric of the air and a stranger stepped through it into the graveyard. He was tall and thin, with red hair cascading round an angular face. Piercing green eyes matched his emerald tunic and he wore a green kilt with a short sword fastened to a thick leather belt.

'The hour grows late,' he said, bowing politely to Charlie. 'Soon humans will begin to enter this place.' His hand whipped out at lightning speed and grabbed the boy's arm—the fingers were impossibly cold and a bone-deep numbness immediately spread from Charlie's elbow to wrist. 'You have done us a

143

great service and you will be treated well, but your fate cannot be altered. You must come with us now.'

Duncan and Peazle looked at each other and hung their heads.

'Take the sword back to Galhadria, highlander,' said the stranger to Duncan. 'That is where we all belong now.'

With a glowering look at the Galhadrian, Duncan bent over, grabbed Excalibur's hilt and pulled. The sword didn't budge. The highlander planted his feet firmly on the ground, put both hands round the handle and pulled until veins stood out on his sinewy arms. He gave up and stepped back, a surprised look on his face.

'It winnae move,' he said.

'What?' The Galhadrian looked at Charlie then back at Excalibur. 'Stay there,' he cautioned and walked round the flat tombstone to where the sword handle protruded from the soil. Charlie looked at the graveyard gate—it was a hundred yards away, half hidden by the church, and he had no doubt the Galhadrian could catch him long before he got there. The stranger was standing over Allan Ramsay's grave now, clutching the sword. Charlie shuffled a few steps towards the flat tombstone and, as he did so, caught Peazle's eye. The pickpocket shook his head slowly, warning the boy not to try anything. Charlie held his gaze. Peazle shook his head again. Charlie shaped his mouth into one unspoken word.

Please.

Peazle bit his lip then sighed and nodded. Duncan had caught the silent exchange and without a change of expression he edged closer to his friend.

The Galhadrian was pulling with all his might on the handle of Excalibur but the sword had not moved an inch. He stood up, the exertion on his face changing into astonishment.

'How did you do this?' he demanded, stepping up onto the flat tomb and towering over the boy. 'What have you done?'

'Now!' shouted Peazle and he and Duncan leapt as one. The boys hit the Galhadrian in a flying tackle and all three tumbled off the tombstone in a tangle of arms and legs. Charlie launched himself forward, cartwheeling over the gravestone and landing in a crouch on the other side. He grabbed the sword handle and pulled Excalibur out of the ground with one fluid motion. The Galhadrian swept Duncan and Peazle away like toys and was on his feet in an instant, his face contorted with rage.

Charlie was pointing the sword at his chest.

'I've already killed one magical creature today,' he snarled. 'Do you want to be the second?'

But the Galhadrian was barely listening—he stood transfixed, staring at the sword in the boy's hand. Duncan and Peazle struggled to their feet looking equally surprised—they had expected Charlie to run for the exit.

'You took the sword from the stone,' the Galhadrian said, awe in his voice. 'When we could not.'

'So what?' Excalibur did not waver in his hand. 'Is this a trick?'

'The sword Excalibur has a power of its own.' The Galhadrian shook his head. 'It will not let us wield it . . . and yet *you* can. I do not understand.'

145

He held up his hand in a gesture of truce. 'Whatever the reason, Excalibur's work obviously is *not* done and neither is yours.'

Charlie snorted. 'Oh, I think I've done all the work I'm going to do for you.'

'That is your choice.' The Galhadrian stepped back. 'But the sword will remain here in case you need it again some day. You may bury it and return to your world—I will not interfere.'

Charlie looked at Peazle and Duncan.

'His word is good,' said Duncan. 'I'll vouch for that, at least.'

The boy lowered Excalibur. The air around the grave had begun to shimmer again.

'Farewell, Master Wilson.' The Galhadrian motioned curtly to Peazle and Duncan. 'Come,' he said brusquely and stepped into the light without a backward glance.

Duncan nodded to the boy.

'Good luck, Charlie,' he said. He hesitated, then reluctantly followed the Galhadrian through the gateway to another land.

Peazle stopped at the entrance to the light.

'Until we meet again, my friend,' he said, doffing his hat.

He stepped through into Galhadria. Charlie saluted him with his sword until the shimmer in the air faded away.

Charlie's mother and father were sitting on the bed and looked up in surprise as their son walked into the room. The boy's hair was matted with dust and grime, his mud-spattered clothes were ripped and dirty and there was a large bloodstain down one side of his shirt.

'What on earth happened to you?' his mother said, eyes wide.

'I've been practising,' the boy replied, plonking himself on the bed between his parents.

'Mum, Dad,' he said putting an arm round each of them. 'I want you to teach me to be an acrobat.'

His parents stared at him and then at each other.

'Well, that's great, Charlie,' his father said, unable to keep the astonishment out of his voice. He patted his son tentatively on the back. 'In fact that's fantastic!'

'We'd be delighted, Charlie.' His mother smiled at him warmly and took his hand. 'There's plenty of stuff to learn, but we'll start whenever you like.'

'Well, I've had a hard day.' The boy let go of his parents, sank back wearily on the bed and closed his eyes. A slow smile spread across his face.

'But tomorrow I think I'll start with a bit of juggling.'

Epilogue

Deep in a cavern, far, far away, a creature stirred—a huge misshapen ear pricking up on its hairless head. From a great distance the cry of her dying brother, born on wind and wave, had wafted down to wreck her slumber.

A tiny glowing eye opened in a mass of white flesh.

Morgana was awake.